"I am your husband, you know."

But that was just it, she thought, she *didn't* know. As far as she was concerned he was a stranger. "I just get the feeling you don't like me very much," she said, before she could stop herself.

"Liking is such a bloodless, insipid emotion. It has nothing to do with what I feel for you."

LEE WILKINSON lives with her husband in England, in a three-hundred-year-old stone cottage in a Derbyshire village, which most winters gets cut off by snow. They both enjoy travel, and recently, joining forces with their daughter and son-in-law, spent a year going around the world "on a shoestring" while their son looked after Kelly, their much-loved German shepherd dog. Lee's hobbies are reading and gardening and holding impromptu barbecues for her long-suffering family and friends.

Lee Wilkinson writes romances with strong heroes and a gripping emotional suspense that will keep you hooked to the very last page!

Books by Lee Wilkinson

HARLEQUIN PRESENTS
1933—THE SECRET MOTHER

Don't miss any of our special offers. Write to us at the following address for information on our newest releases.

Harlequin Reader Service
U.S.: 3010 Walden Ave., P.O. Box 1325, Buffalo, NY 14269
Canadian: P.O. Box 609, Fort Erie, Ont. L2A 5X3

LEE WILKINSON

A Husband's Revenge

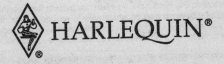

TORONTO • NEW YORK • LONDON
AMSTERDAM • PARIS • SYDNEY • HAMBURG
STOCKHOLM • ATHENS • TOKYO • MILAN • MADRID
PRAGUE • WARSAW • BUDAPEST • AUCKLAND

ISBN 0-373-11991-7

A HUSBAND'S REVENGE

First North American Publication 1998.

CHAPTER ONE

SHE opened her eyes to a strange, underwater world of light and shade. After a moment her blurred vision cleared and she found herself looking at a bare, impersonal room, little more than a cubicle.

The walls and ceiling were painted sickly green; the floor covering was grey rubberised tiles. A metal locker and a wheeled trolley stood next to a white porcelain sink, where a tap dripped with monotonous regularity.

There were no curtains at the window, and bright sunshine slanted in. It was the only cheerful thing in the room. A panacea. Something to be filtered in between the fear and the smell of disinfectant.

She was wearing a much washed blue cotton gown that fastened down the back with tapes and lying on a hard, narrow bed. A hospital bed. It made no sense. Too tired to try and think, she closed her eyes once more.

The next time she awoke the sunshine had gone and dusk had taken its place. Shadows gathered in the room like a menacing crowd. Her throat was dry, her mouth parched. The tap was still dripping, and there was a red plastic beaker on the sink.

Pushing herself up on one elbow, she swung her bare feet to the floor. But when she straightened and attempted to take a step her head swam, and she was forced to hang onto the metal bar at the top of the bed.

At the same instant the door opened to admit a young and pretty dark-haired nurse, who hurried over and, after helping her patient back into the high bed, scolded, 'You shouldn't be trying to get out on your own.'

'I'm thirsty.' The words were just a croak.

'Well, stay where you are and I'll get you some nice cool orange juice.' She plumped up the thin pillows and switched on a harsh overhead light. 'The doctor will be pleased you're awake at last.'

Awake… Yes, she was awake. Yet it was as if her brain was still asleep. She was conscious of physical things—her head ached dully and her throat felt as if it was full of hot shards of glass—but she was dazed and disorientated, her mind a curious blank.

The nurse returned and handed her the promised glass of orange juice. While she drank eagerly there was a flurry of footsteps, and a short sandy-haired man hurried in. He wore a white coat, steel-rimmed glasses and an air of harassed self-importance.

Pulling a pencil-torch from his pocket, he shone it into her eyes before taking her pulse. Then, sitting down on the bed, he informed her, 'My name's Hauser. I'm the doctor in charge.'

His complexion was pasty, and he appeared so effete that he would have made a better patient, she decided wryly, and asked, 'In charge of what?'

Judging from his look of disapproval, he thought she was being facetious.

'I mean, what is this place?' Her voice was husky.

'The accident and emergency wing of the charity hospital.'

'Have I had an accident?'

'You were brought in earlier today by a cabby. He says you stepped off the sidewalk in front of him. His fender caught you and you fell and hit your head. As far as we can tell, you have no injuries other than minor bruising and slight concussion. Unfortunately you weren't carrying any means of identification, so we were unable to notify your next of kin.'

He made it sound as if she'd planned the whole thing just to annoy and inconvenience both him and the nursing staff.

'This is a very busy hospital, and it gets busier late at night. Especially at the weekend.' Having made that point, he headed for the door, saying over his shoulder, 'If you'll give the nurse details of who you are and where you live, we'll contact your family so someone can come and collect you.'

'But I don't know where I live...'

The forlorn statement brought him back.

'You've had a shock. Try and think. Are you a tourist?'

'A tourist? I don't know.'

'Do you remember your name?'

'No... I don't remember *anything*... Oh, dear God!'

'Don't worry.' He became a little more human. 'Temporary amnesia isn't uncommon after your kind of accident. It just means you'll have to stay.' His frown made it clear that this wasn't a popular option. 'Until either you regain your memory or someone misses you and checks the hospitals.'

Temporary amnesia. As the door closed behind him and the nurse began to make notes on her chart she did her best to cling to that thought, but a rising panic fought its way to the surface. 'I don't know if there's anyone to *make* enquiries... I don't know if I've *got* any family...'

A terrible sense of desolation swept over her. She covered her face with her hands. Her skin felt too tight for her bones, her cheeks and jaw all angles and sharp lines. 'I don't even know what I *look* like.'

Opening the locker, the nurse brought out a grubby,

finger-marked mirror and handed it to her. 'Well, at least that should cheer you up.'

A pale, heart-shaped face surrounded by a cloud of dark silky hair stared back at her. There was an ugly purple bruise spreading over her right temple. Almond-shaped eyes, a short, straight nose, high, slanting cheekbones and a disproportionately wide mouth, the lips of which looked bloodless, did little to cheer her.

The blue eyes, so deep they looked violet, and the fine, clear skin, seemed to be her best features. Well, my girl, you're no beauty, she told herself silently as she handed back the mirror.

Looking down at her hands, she saw they were slim and shapely, the oval nails free of polish, the fingers bare of rings.

She felt a peculiar relief.

When the nurse had rinsed the glass and refilled it with tap water, she said, 'It looks as if you'll be here for the night at least, so would you like a little supper?'

'No, thank you. I'm not hungry.'

'Then get some sleep. Perhaps by morning your memory will have come back.' Switching off the light, the nurse departed.

Oh, if only! It was *terrifying*, this feeling of being lost, isolated in a black void. She lay for what seemed hours, trying fruitlessly to shed some light on who she was and where she'd come from, before finally falling asleep.

Some time later she woke with a start, hugging her pillow in a death grip.

Someone was just closing the door. Failing to latch, it swung open a few inches, letting a crack of light spill into the room from the corridor.

'I've no intention of waiting until morning.' Just outside the door a masculine voice spoke clearly, decisively.

Sounding flustered, the nurse said, 'We don't normally release patients this late.'

'I'm sure you could make an exception.'

'Well, you'd have to speak to Dr Hauser.'

'Very well.'

They began to move away.

'I couldn't let her go without his permission, and I'm not sure if... Oh, here he is...'

Though she could still hear the murmur of conversation, the actual words were no longer clear. After a minute or two the voices came closer, apparently returning.

Dr Hauser was saying, 'We certainly need the bed, but I'm afraid I can't allow—'

That authoritative voice cut in crisply. 'I want her out of this place. Now!'

Stiffly, the doctor said, 'I have my patient's welfare to consider, and I really don't think—'

'Look—' this time the tone was more moderate, the impatience curbed '—I'm aware you do some very good work here. I'm also well aware that this kind of charity hospital is always drastically underfunded...'

There was a pause and a rustle. 'Here's a cheque made out to the hospital. It's blank at the moment. If you'll make the necessary arrangements for her immediate release, I'll be happy to make a substantial contribution towards the hospital's running costs.'

Sounding mollified, the doctor said, 'Will you step into my office for a moment?' and three pairs of footsteps moved away.

Sitting up against her pillows, torn between hope and anxiety, she waited. Was this someone come for her? If it was, and please God it was, surely a familiar face would bring her memory back?

It seemed an age before one set of footsteps returned and the door swung wider. 'Ah, you're awake. Good.'

The doctor switched on the shaded night-light. 'Have you remembered anything?'

Her throat moved as she swallowed. 'No.'

He came to sit on the edge of the bed. 'Well, you'll be pleased to know you've been identified as Clare Saunders...'

The name meant nothing to her.

'And you're English. That accounts for the accent.'

Of course she was English. Yet both the nurse and doctor had *American* accents. That fact hadn't really registered until now, almost as if subconsciously she'd *expected* to hear American accents... 'But I've never been to the States.' She spoke the thought aloud.

'You mean until you came to live here?'

'I live in England.' Of that she was sure.

'At the moment you're living here in New York.'

'*New York!* No, I can't *possibly* be living in New York.' For some reason the idea scared her witless. 'You must have got the wrong person.'

He shook his head. 'You're Mrs Clare Saunders. Your husband has given us definite proof of your identity.'

'My *husband!* But I haven't got a husband!' That was something else she was sure of. 'I'm not married!'

Reacting to the note of rising hysteria in her voice, Dr Hauser said sharply, 'Now, try to stay calm. Amnesia can be extremely upsetting, but it should only be a matter of time before your memory returns in full.'

'What if it doesn't?'

'In the vast majority of cases it *does*,' he said a shade irritably. 'Believe me, Mrs Saunders, you have nothing to fear. We are quite satisfied—both with your husband's identity and with yours. We're prepared to let you leave at once, and as soon as Mr Saunders has signed the papers that release you into his care, he'll be here.'

What would have been good news a short time ago

was all at once terrifying. If only she didn't have to go *tonight*. By tomorrow her memory might have returned.

She caught at the doctor's arm. 'Oh, please, can't I stay until morning?' But even as she begged she sensed there was no help to be had from that quarter.

'Do you know where this hospital is situated?'

'No.' It was just a whisper.

'This downtown area is rough,' he told her. 'Late at night we get a lot of drunks and people injured in brawls. You obviously don't belong in a place like this, and I can't blame your husband for wanting to take you home without delay.'

He patted her hand. 'Don't forget, all your doubts will be set at rest if you recognise him.'

And if she *didn't*?

But the doctor was satisfied, and that was all there was to it. If he hadn't been, despite the contribution to the hospital's funds—she closed her mind to the word 'bribe'—he wouldn't have released her.

Or would he?

The door swung open and a tall, dark-haired, broad-shouldered man strode in. He was very well dressed, but it was his easy air of power and authority, his natural arrogance, that proclaimed him top of the heap.

As if by right he took the doctor's place on the edge of the bed. He appeared to be in his early thirties, his face was lean and tough, and his handsome black-pupilled eyes were a light, clear green beneath curved brows.

He was a complete stranger.

As though mesmerised, she found herself staring at his mouth. The upper lip was thin, the lower fuller, and with a slight dip in the centre that echoed the cleft in his chin. It was an austere, yet sensual mouth—a mouth that was at once beautiful and ruthless.

Suddenly she shivered.

Those brilliant eyes searched her face, apparently looking for some sign of recognition. When he found none, his own face hardened, as though with anger, but his voice was soft as he said, 'Clare, darling...I've been nearly frantic.'

Then, as without conscious volition she shrank away, he said, 'It's Jos... Surely you remember me? I'm your husband.'

If he was, why did she feel this instinctive fear of him? And why did she get the impression that he was cloaking his displeasure, playing the part of a loving husband to satisfy Dr Hauser?

He took her hand.

In a reflex action she snatched it away, cradling it against her chest as though he'd hurt it.

'You're not my husband! I know you're not.' Turning to the doctor, she cried desperately, 'I've never *seen* him before!' She held out her left hand. 'Look, I'm not even wearing a ring.'

The man who called himself Jos felt in his pocket and produced a wide band of chased gold and a huge diamond solitaire. 'You took your rings off when you showered this morning and forgot to put them back.'

No, she didn't believe him. Somehow she knew she wasn't the kind of woman who would lightly remove her wedding ring.

As she began to shake her head he caught her hand, and, holding it with delicate cruelty when she would have pulled it free, slipped both rings onto her slender finger. 'See? A perfect fit.'

He gave her a cool, implacable stare, which sent a quiver of apprehension through her, before lifting her hand to his lips and kissing the palm. 'And if you want further proof that we're married...' Removing a marriage certificate and a couple of snapshots from his wallet, he held them out to her.

A marriage certificate might be anyone's, so she didn't even bother to look at it, but photographs couldn't lie. Afraid of what she might see, she forced herself to take the Polaroid pictures and look at them.

The first one had been taken in what appeared to be a cottage garden. She was smiling up at a tall, dark-haired attractive man. His arm was around her waist and she looked radiantly happy.

'That was the day we got engaged...and that was our wedding day.'

The second picture showed a couple just emerging from the stone porch of a village church. Dressed in an ivory satin bridal gown and holding a spray of pale pink rosebuds, she was on the arm of the same man, who now wore a well-cut grey suit with a white carnation in his buttonhole.

A man who was undoubtedly Jos.

'Do you still believe we're not married?'

She couldn't deny the evidence of her own eyes, but she knew that no matter what the picture suggested she didn't *want* to be married to this man.

'Well, Clare?'

'No.' It was just a whisper.

Standing in the background, Dr Hauser nodded his approval just as his bleeper summoned him. 'I must go. Try not to worry, Mrs Saunders. I'm sure your loss of memory will prove to be only temporary.'

The door had hardly closed behind him when there was a bump and it swung open again to admit the nurse, pushing a shabby wheelchair. 'Well, isn't this good news?' she asked her patient cheerfully. 'As soon as you're dressed, you can go home.'

Taking a small pile of clothing from the locker, she

pulled back the bed-sheet and the single greyish cellular blanket. 'Shall I give you a hand with the gown? Or would you prefer your husband to help you?'

Jos eyed the hospital gown with distaste, and raised an enquiring brow.

Agitated, because she was naked beneath the faded cotton and he knew it, Clare folded her arms across her chest and hugged herself defensively. 'No, I...I don't need any help.'

He rose to his feet in one lithe movement and said smoothly, 'Then I'll wait outside.'

'You didn't remember him?' the nurse queried, unfastening the tapes.

Clare shook her head mutely.

'So I guess you're entitled to be shy. Though I'd have thought a man like that would have been impossible to forget. He's really *something*...'

Seeing nothing else for it, Clare swung her legs off the bed and stood up. Moving slowly, carefully, wincing as she touched her bruised ribs, she began to get dressed in clothes she didn't even recognise as hers.

The undies were pretty and delicate, the silky suit and sandals well-chosen and smart, but all of them appeared to be relatively cheap. Which didn't seem to tie in with *his* expensive clothes.

Her tongue loosened, the nurse was chattering on. 'I must say I envy you. It's so thrilling and exciting. Like meeting for the first time and falling in love all over again...'

Clare wished she could see things in such a romantic light. Caught between an unknown future with a man who was a stranger to her and a blank past, all she could feel was alarm and dread.

All too soon she was dressed. With no further excuse for dawdling she took a few steps and, feeling weak, found herself glad to sink into the wheelchair the nurse was holding for her.

Standing at ease, showing no sign of impatience now, Jos was waiting in the bare corridor. He was very tall, six feet three or four, with wide shoulders and narrow hips.

He looked hard and handsome. And somehow dangerous.

Though he was so big, when he came towards them she saw he moved with the grace and agility of a man perfectly in control of his body.

'Shall I come down with you?' the nurse asked.

Anxious to put off the time when she'd be left alone with him, Clare was about to accept the offer when he said pleasantly, 'Thank you, but there's really no need. I'm sure I can handle a wheelchair.'

The smile accompanying his words held such devastating charm that the nurse almost swooned. She was still standing staring after them when they reached the lift.

It came promptly at his summons.

It probably didn't dare do anything else, Clare found herself thinking as the doors slid open. Then she was trapped with him in a small steel box. It was a relief when it stopped a few floors down and a hospital porter got in pushing a trolley.

As the doctor had predicted, things were hotting up. The main concourse was busy and bustling, with people and staff milling about.

At the reception desk a hard-pressed woman was trying to cope with a growing queue. A large calendar with a picture of Cape Cod on it proclaimed the month was June.

When they reached an area close to the entrance, where a straggling row of shabby wheelchairs jostled each other, Jos asked, 'Can you manage to walk from here?' His deep, incisive voice startled her. 'Or shall I carry you?'

The idea of being held against that broad chest startled her even more. Sharply, she said, 'Of course I can walk.' They were foolhardy words that she was soon to regret.

Struggling out of the chair, ignoring the hand he held out, she added, 'I've only lost my memory, not the use of my legs,' and saw his lips tighten ominously.

Once on her feet, Clare swayed a little, and he put a steady arm around her waist. As soon as she regained her balance she pulled away, leaving a good foot of space between them.

His face cold and aloof, he walked by her side, making no further attempt to touch her.

Somehow she managed to keep her chin high and her spine ramrod-straight, but, legs trembling, head curiously light and hot, just to put one foot in front of the other took a tremendous effort of will.

His car was quite close, parked in a 'Doctors Only' area. A sleek silvery grey, it had that unmistakable air of luxury possessed only by the most expensive of vehicles.

By the time he'd unlocked and opened the passenger door she was enveloped in a cold sweat and her head had started to whirl. Eyes closed, she leaned against the car.

Muttering, 'Stubborn little fool!' he caught her beneath the arms and lowered her into the seat. A moment later he slid in beside her and leaned over to fasten her safety belt.

'Have you had anything to eat?' he demanded.

As soon as she was sitting down the faintness began to pass and the world stopped spinning. Lifting her head, she answered, 'I wasn't hungry.'

'No wonder you look like a ghost!'

Knowing it was as much emotional exhaustion as physical, she said helplessly, 'It's not just that. It's *everything*.'

He started the car and drove to the entrance, giving way to a small ambulance with blue flashing lights before turning uptown.

The dashboard clock told her it was two-thirty in the morning, and, apart from the ubiquitous yellow cabs and a few late revellers, the streets of New York were relatively quiet though as bright as day.

Above the streetlamps and the lighted shop windows, by contrast it looked black—black towers of glass and concrete rising into a black sky.

It was totally strange. Alien.

As though sensing her shiver, he remarked more moderately, 'Waking up with amnesia must be distressing.'

'It is,' she said simply. 'Not to know *who* you are, *where* you are, where you're *going*—and I mean *know* rather than just being *told*—is truly terrifying.'

'I can imagine.' He sounded almost sympathetic.

'At first you just seemed to be…angry…' She struggled to put her earlier impression into words. 'As if you blamed me in some way…'

'It's been rather a fraught day… And I wasn't convinced your loss of memory was genuine.'

'You thought I was making it up! Why on earth should I do a thing like that?'

'Why does a woman do anything?' he asked bitterly.

It appeared that he didn't think much of women in general and her in particular.

'But I would have had to have some *reason*, surely?'

After a slight hesitation, he said evasively, 'It's irrelevant as you *have* lost your memory.'

'What makes you believe it now when you didn't earlier?'

They stopped at a red light and he turned his head to study her. 'Because you have a kind of poignant, lost look that would be almost impossible to fake.'

'I still don't understand why you think I'd *want* to fake it.'

He gave her a cool glance. 'Perhaps to get a little of your own back.' Then, as if conceding that some further explanation was needed, he went on, 'We'd quarrelled. I had to go out. When I came back I found you'd gone off in a huff.'

Instinctively she glanced down at her left hand.

'Yes—' his eyes followed hers '—that was why you weren't wearing your rings.'

It must have been some quarrel to make her take her wedding ring off. She racked her brains, trying to remember.

Nothing.

Giving up the attempt, she asked, 'What did we quarrel about?'

For an instant he looked discomposed, then, as the lights turned to green and the car moved smoothly forward, he replied, 'As with most quarrels, it began over something comparatively unimportant. But somehow it escalated.'

She was about to point out that he hadn't really answered her question when he forestalled her.

'I can't see much sense in raking over the ashes. As soon as your memory returns you'll be able to judge for yourself how trivial it was. Now I suggest that you try and relax. Let things come back in their own good time rather than keep asking questions.'

Questions he didn't want to answer?

Yet if not, why not? Unless he didn't *want* her to regain her memory?

Helplessly, she said, 'But there's so much I don't know. I don't even know where I...we...live.'

'Upper East Side.'

That figured. It went with his obvious wealth, his air of good breeding, his educated accent. She frowned. *His accent*... Basically an English accent?

'You're not American?'

'I was born in England.'

'How long have you been in the States?'

'Since I was twenty-one.'

'How old are you now?'

'Thirty.'

'Do your family still live in England?'

Glancing at his handsome profile, she saw his jaw tighten before, his voice repressive, he replied, 'I haven't any family.'

Plainly he was in no mood to be questioned. But, needing to know more about this stranger she was married to, about their life together, she persisted, 'Where did we meet...?'

He swung the wheel and they turned into a paved forecourt and drew to a halt in front of a huge apartment block.

'Was it in England?'

Curtly, he said, 'I thought I'd made it clear that I wanted you to rest rather than keep asking questions.'

Resenting the way he was treating her, she protested, 'But I—'

He put a finger to her lips. 'This is the Ventnor Building and we're home. Any further questions will keep until tomorrow.'

The light pressure of that lean finger against her

mouth stopped her breath and made her lower lip start to tremble.

Watching her with hooded eyes, he moved it slowly, tracing the lovely, passionate outline of her mouth, and she was submerged by a wave of sensation so strong that it scared her half to death.

She saw his white teeth gleam in a smile, and suddenly felt terribly vulnerable. He knew only too well what effect his touch had on her.

As he got out and came round to open her door a blue-uniformed night-security guard appeared from nowhere.

'Mr Saunders, Mrs Saunders...' He gave them a laconic salute. 'Want me to park her for you?'

'Please, Bill.' Jos tossed him the keys and stooped to help Clare from the car. With a strong arm around her waist he led her past the main doors to a side entrance and slid a card into the lock.

The chandelier-lit marble foyer, ringed by glittering stores and boutiques, was vast and empty. Their footsteps echoed eerily in the silence as, watched by the glassy eyes of the elegantly dressed mannequins in the shop windows, they crossed to a bank of elevators.

He produced a key, and a moment later the doors of his private elevator slid to behind them.

'You live in the penthouse.' Her own certainty surprised her.

Brilliant eyes narrowed to slits, he turned to watch her like a hawk, his hard face all planes and angles. 'What makes you so sure?'

As they shot smoothly upwards she pressed her fingers to her temples and struggled to pin down the elusive recollection. It was like trying to trace one particular shadow in a room full of shadows.

She shook her head. 'I don't know.'

They slid to a halt, and with a hand beneath her elbow he led her across a luxuriously carpeted hall and into an elegant living room. The room must be on a corner of the building, she realised, because two walls at right angles seemed to be made entirely of lightly smoked glass panels which opened onto a terrace and roof garden.

She could see the shapes of trees and bushes and hear the splash of a fountain. It seemed strange when they were so far above the city.

With some trepidation, she said, 'I think I'm scared of heights.'

'Then perhaps you shouldn't have chosen to marry a man who lives in a penthouse.'

With a sudden sensation of *déjà vu*, she felt sure he'd said those mocking words to her once before, used the same coolly cutting tone.

Though unable to recall the precise terms of their relationship, she was certain it wasn't of the pleasant, friendly 'rub along together' sort, but rather the tempestuous 'strike sparks off each other' kind.

The kind where someone could get hurt.

No, not someone. *Her*. Every instinct warned her that Jos was dangerous, that he wanted to hurt her, would *enjoy* hurting her.

'Why do you want to hurt me?' The question was out before she could prevent it.

'Why should I want to hurt you?'

Glancing quickly at him, she saw his dark face was cool and shuttered. It would only reveal what he wanted it to reveal. He would only tell her what he wanted her to know.

'What makes you imagine I want to hurt you?' he persisted.

She made a helpless gesture with her hands. 'I don't

know. I just get the feeling you don't like me very much.'

He moved towards her.

Instinctively she backed away.

Reaching out, he caught her wrist and pulled her against him. One arm held her while his free hand came up to encircle her throat lightly.

Something about his stillness, the tension in his muscles, warned her that he was waiting for her to struggle.

When she stood as if frozen, he bent his dark head and let his lips wander over her cheek and jaw. She caught her breath, aware of the faint scent of his skin, the slight roughness of stubble.

His lips brushed her ear, making her shiver, as he said, 'Liking is such a bloodless, insipid emotion. It has nothing to do with what I feel for you.'

Recognising something fundamental in his words, knowing she was close to an important truth, she felt her heart begin to race with suffocating speed. 'What *do* you feel for me?'

The sudden flare of anger in his eyes made her blood run cold. Before she could do or say anything he covered her mouth with his own.

While he deepened the kiss, ravaging her mouth with a savage, punitive expertise, she lay against him, lost and dazed, knowing only that if he released his grip she would fall.

When he finally lifted his head she was trembling in every limb, her breath coming in harsh gasps.

He looked down at her, studying the violet eyes that looked too big for her heart-shaped face, the swollen lips, the fine dew of perspiration on her forehead, and said tightly, 'You should know better than to try to provoke me.'

'I wasn't trying to provoke you,' she denied in a husky whisper.

With a muttered oath he let her go so suddenly that she staggered a little, and the beautiful room whirled sickeningly around her head.

A moment later he had swept her up in his arms and was carrying her into what was obviously the master bedroom.

'What are you doing?' she croaked.

'Taking you to bed.'

'No!' Every trace of colour drained from her face, leaving it ashen.

Setting her on her feet, he said coldly, 'Credit me with *some* sensitivity. I can see you've had about as much stress as you can handle, so for tonight at least I'll sleep in the guest room.'

She gave the kind of shuddering sigh a child might give.

The impatience dying out of his face, he opened one of the drawers and tossed her an ivory satin nightgown with shoestring straps and a matching negligee. 'Do you need any help?'

'No!' she snapped, then added more moderately, 'No, thank you.'

'You'll find your toilet things in the bathroom. I'll give you ten minutes.'

In the big, luxurious bathroom, hurrying as much as her debilitating weakness would allow, she pulled off her clothes and dropped them into the dirty linen basket, showered, cleaned her teeth and dragged a brush through her damp hair.

She was safely in bed, leaning against the pillows, the lightweight duvet pulled chest-high, when he returned.

Sitting on the edge of the king-sized divan, he handed

her a beaker of hot chocolate. 'Drink that before I tuck you in.'

The smell made her wrinkle her nose. 'I don't like hot chocolate.'

'Drink it all the same. It'll help you sleep soundly.'

Sipping obediently, she avoided his eyes.

As soon as the beaker was empty he put it on the bedside cabinet and then, rising to his feet, reached to flatten her pillows.

As she slid down his hand brushed her breast and she flinched away.

His chiselled mouth tightened. 'There's no need to look quite so alarmed. I am your husband, you know.'

But that was just it, she thought as the door closed behind him, she *didn't* know. As far as she was concerned he was a stranger.

But a stranger who had a devastating effect on her.

Earlier, when he'd kissed her, desire, terrifying in its intensity, had overwhelmed her. And, though his intention had clearly been to punish her, she'd sensed a fierce reciprocal hunger in him, which even such a cold, self-controlled man as he couldn't totally hide.

Their relationship, whatever other dark threads were woven into it, was undoubtedly a passionate one.

Suddenly she was even more afraid of what the future held than she had been when she'd left the hospital.

CHAPTER TWO

CLARE'S brain stirred into life slowly, unwillingly. Lying stretched on her back, eyes closed, she was aware of softness and warmth, of a physical comfort that went hand in hand with a kind of bleak mental anguish.

Bodily she was at ease, but her mind was a teeming mass of disturbing, shadowy thoughts. When she tried to hold onto them, to coax them into the light, they vanished like wraiths, leaving only a set of hard, handsome features indelibly printed there.

Jos. Her husband.

Her heart began to beat at a fast, suffocating speed. She recalled him coming to the hospital. Bringing her home. Kissing her. Innocuous enough memories except for the powerful black undercurrents which, like some deadly whirlpool, threatened to drag her down and drown her.

Undercurrents which, if she could only remember, would almost certainly explain why she had taken off her rings and walked out in the first place.

But had she just stormed off in a temper, as he'd tried to imply? Or had she meant to go for good?

If she *had* meant to leave him, surely she would have taken a case? Certainly she would have had a handbag. Some money…

Eyelids still closed, to help her concentration, she tried to think, but her memory would go back no further than awakening in the hospital.

Sighing, she opened her eyes to semi-gloom. Abruptly the sigh turned into a gasp. The sight of Jos lounging in a chair by the bed, his eyes fixed on her face, made her jerk upright.

His mere presence brought a surge of dismay and excitement that took her breath and made her heart start to race again.

As though he'd run restless fingers through it, his hair, peat-dark, not quite black, was slightly rumpled, his jaw was smooth, clean-shaven, his lean face, with its fascinating planes and angles, heart-stoppingly attractive.

He was casually dressed in light trousers and a dark green cotton-knit shirt open at the neck, exposing his tanned throat, and with the sleeves pushed up his muscular hair-sprinkled forearms.

Pulling the duvet high, though her nightgown was perfectly modest, she demanded hoarsely, 'How long have you been there?'

His clearly delineated mouth curved slightly. 'Most of the afternoon.'

The idea of him sitting watching her sleep was disturbing, to say the least. Slowly, with an effort, she smoothed her face into a careful, unrevealing mask, before asking, 'Why didn't you wake me?'

Rising to his feet, he crossed to the wide window and drew aside the curtains, flooding the attractive blue and white room with light, before answering, 'I wanted you to wake up naturally. I thought perhaps...?' He allowed the question to tail off.

'It's no use...' She heard the desolation of her own despair. 'I can't remember anything prior to waking up in the hospital.'

Suddenly he was by her side again, looming too close. Tilting her chin, he examined her face, taking in the translucent skin stretched tightly over the wonderful bone structure, the paleness of her lips, the lost look in the long-lashed violet eyes.

His touch closed her throat and made her mouth go dry. Unconsciously, she ran the tip of her tongue over parched lips.

Something flaring in his green eyes, he followed the small, betraying movement. She froze, terrified he was going to kiss her, *wanting* him to kiss her...

He, who seemed never to miss a thing, obviously noted her reaction and smiled a little. Releasing her chin, he touched a bell by the bedhead before sitting down again. 'When you say "anything"...?'

It took her a moment or two to recover. Then, forehead creased in thought, she said slowly, 'I remember the ordinary everyday things of life. How to read and write, add up and subtract...that kind of thing. It's *personal* memories that have gone...'

Were those memories so dark, so disturbing, that her subconscious *wanted* them blanked out? Had she *needed* to lose herself and the past in order to survive some emotional trauma?

Or was this feeling of being threatened by past and future alike merely symptomatic of her amnesia? When her memory returned would she find she was a perfectly ordinary woman with a perfectly ordinary marriage?

But suppose it *never* returned?

Fighting down a rush of blind panic at the thought, she went on, 'I don't know anything about myself. If I've got a middle name or what my maiden name was... I don't even know how old I am.'

'Your middle name is Linden, your maiden name was Berkeley and you're twenty-four. You'll be twenty-five on September the third. A Virgo,' he added, with a derisive twist to his lips.

Before Clare could react to what seemed to be a sneer,

there was a tap at the door, and it opened to admit a dark-suited dignified man, carrying a tray. Pulling the metal supports into position, he placed it carefully across her knees.

Bending his balding head deferentially, he said, 'I'm delighted that madam is safely home.'

'Thank you, er…' She hesitated.

'This is Roberts,' Jos informed her. Then, to the man-servant, he said, 'I'm afraid Mrs Saunders still hasn't recovered her memory.'

Roberts looked suitably grave. 'Very upsetting for both of you, sir.'

After deftly removing the lid from a dish of poached salmon, he opened and shook out a white damask nap-kin. 'Mr Saunders thought a light meal… If, however, madam would prefer chicken, or an omelette…?'

'Oh, no… Thank you.' Then, sensing a genuine wish to please, she remarked with a smile, 'I'm sure this will be delicious.'

Roberts departed noiselessly.

'A butler instead of a housekeeper?' Sipping her tea, Clare spoke her thoughts aloud. 'I get the feeling you don't care much for women?'

'In one area at least I find a woman is indispensable.' His mocking glance left her in no doubt as to which area he referred to. 'I also employ a couple of female cleaners. But I happen to prefer a male servant to run the household.'

Head bent, hoping to hide her blush, she asked, 'Has Roberts been with you long?'

'He came with the penthouse.' Then, with no change of tone, he added, 'Your salmon will get cold.'

Uncomfortably, she asked, 'Aren't you eating?'

'I had a late lunch a couple of hours ago, when it

appeared that you were still in shock and were going to sleep the clock round.'

She glanced at her bare left wrist before asking, 'What time is it now?'

'Nearly four-thirty.' Lifting her hand, making the huge diamond solitaire flash in the light, he asked, 'Do you remember what happened to your watch?'

'Do I usually wear one?'

'Yes. So far as I know, always.' Letting go of her hand, he urged, 'Do eat something or you'll upset Roberts.'

Feeling suddenly ravenous, Clare began to tuck in with a will. Glancing up to find Jos's eyes were watching her every move, she hesitated.

'Don't let me put you off,' he said abruptly. 'You must be starving. It's over twenty-four hours since you were knocked down.'

Glancing once again at her empty wrist, she suggested, 'Perhaps I left my watch behind when I...with my rings...'

He shook his head emphatically. 'You wouldn't have left it behind.' Dark face thoughtful, he went on, 'When you arrived at the hospital you had no handbag with you. Didn't you think that was strange? Don't most women carry a bag?'

Putting down her knife and fork, she agreed, 'Yes, I suppose so.'

'It's my belief that when you were knocked down, by the time the cabby had pulled himself together and got out, your bag and watch had been stolen. It's a pretty rough area... Have you any idea what you were doing there?'

'No.' Then, harking back, she asked curiously, 'What makes you so sure I wouldn't have left my watch behind?'

He rose to his feet and, lifting the tray from her knees, set it aside before answering, 'Because it was a twenty-first birthday gift from your parents.'

'My parents?' Her heart suddenly lifted with hope. 'Where do they—?'

'They're dead,' he said harshly, resuming his seat. 'They died in a plane crash in Panama a few months ago.'

'Oh…' She felt a curious hollowness, an emptiness that grief should have filled. 'Did you know them?'

After an almost imperceptible hesitation, he said, 'I knew of them.'

'Can you tell me anything about them?' she asked eagerly. 'Anything that might help me to remember? Our family background…where they lived?'

This time he hesitated so long that she found herself wondering anew if he would prefer her *not* to remember.

Then, as though making up his mind, he said, 'Yes, I can tell you about your family background.' His face hard, his green eyes curiously angry, he went on, 'Your father was Sir Roger Berkeley, your mother, Lady Isobel Berkeley. He was a diplomat and she was a well-known hostess, prominent in fashionable society.'

Clare could sense an underlying tension in his manner, a marked bitterness.

'You were born and brought up in a house called Stratton Place, a mile or so from Meredith.'

'Meredith?'

'A pretty little village not too far from London. A lot of rich people live there—bankers, stockbrokers, politicians… You went to an expensive boarding-school until you were eighteen, then a Swiss finishing-school.'

He sounded as if he resented their wealth and position, and she wondered briefly if he'd come from a poorer environment. But that didn't tally with his voice and his educated accent.

'You were an only child—and a mistake, I fancy.'

Chilled both by the concept and Jos's deliberate cruelty, she asked, 'How could you know a thing like that?'

He shrugged broad shoulders. 'I'm judging by the type of woman your mother was, and the fact that you were pushed off to boarding-school at a very early age...'

Clare felt impelled to defend the mother she couldn't remember. 'But are you in a position to judge? If you didn't really know her...'

'I know all I need to know. When your father was posted to the States she joined him in New York. The society gossip columns had a field-day. Men swarmed round her like flies, and she soon got quite a reputation as a goer...' There was contempt in the deep voice. Softly, he added, 'You're very like her.'

Every trace of colour draining from her face, she sat quite still. Surely she couldn't be the kind of woman he was describing?

Watching her expressive face mirror her consternation, he allowed a scornful little smile to play around his lips.

In response to that smile, she lifted her chin. No, she refused to believe it. Some fundamental self-knowledge told her he must be wrong.

'I can't answer for my mother,' she said calmly, 'but I'm sure *I'm* not like that.'

'You're the image of her in looks...'

'That doesn't necessarily make me *like* her.'

As though she hadn't spoken, he went on, 'You both have the kind of beauty that can drive any man wild.'

Clare shook her head. 'When I woke in the hospital I

had no idea what I looked like. The nurse gave me a mirror. I'm not even pretty.'

'You're far more than pretty. You're fascinating. Wholly bewitching.'

But the way he spoke the words made them a damning indictment rather than a compliment.

A shiver ran through her. 'I didn't bewitch you,' she said with certainty.

His voice brittle as ice crystals, he contradicted her. 'Oh, but my darling, you did.'

She didn't believe it for one moment. Almost in despair, she asked, 'Why did you marry me?'

'Why do you think?'

'I don't know. If I'm like my mother—' She broke off in confusion.

'You mean it wouldn't have been necessary?' He smiled like a tiger. 'If I'd only wanted a casual affair, it wouldn't have been.'

He spoke with such certainty that her blood turned to ice in her veins.

'But I wanted a great deal more than that...'

Without knowing why, she shivered. 'So what *did* you want?' Perhaps she needed to hear him put it into words, like some *coup de grâce*.

His mouth smiled, but his eyes were cold as green glass. 'I wanted to own you body and soul.'

She shivered again. Then slowly, almost as if in accusation, she said, 'You didn't love me.'

With no reason to dissemble, he told her matter-of-factly, 'I never pretended to. On the contrary, I went to great lengths not to mention the word "love", so there would be no possibility that you could have any illusions, be under any misapprehension...'

Filled with a lost, bleak emptiness that was far worse than anything she had yet experienced, she accepted the fact that he had never loved her and she must have been aware of that.

Then why had she married him?

Recalling the overwhelming effect his kisses had had on her, one reason immediately sprang to mind. Yet surely common sense would have prevented her marrying a man simply because he attracted her physically?

Unless that attraction had developed into an infatuation and, more like her mother than she wanted to believe, she'd been unable to help herself...

'And neither was I...' Jos was going on, his voice like polished steel. 'I knew perfectly well why you agreed to marry me.'

Shrinking inwardly at the realisation that her sexual enslavement must have been obvious, she waited for him to crow.

Incredibly, he said, 'I was wealthy, and you wanted a rich husband.'

At that moment all she could feel was relief. The fact that he didn't realise how obsessed she must have been went some way towards salving her pride.

'Someone who could give you the right kind of lifestyle.'

'It's my impression that I already had that.' Somehow she kept her voice steady.

'Ah, but you didn't. When you left your smart finishing-school, for some reason—you never told me exactly what—you struck out on your own. You rented a small cottage in the village and took a job in a real estate office while you waited for the opportunity to catch a suitable husband.'

'Did I tell you that?' she asked sharply.

'You didn't need to.'

'And I suppose by "suitable" you mean...?'

'Stinking rich.' He spoke bitterly. 'Because of the

kind of life your parents led—jet-setting, champagne parties, lots of entertaining—they always lived above their income, and I suppose you must have realised there'd be nothing left when they died. Therefore, you needed to hook a man with money.'

The picture he was painting of her was a far from pleasant one. Pushing back a tendril of dark silky hair, she objected, 'If I was an ordinary working girl, what chance would I have had of ever meeting any rich men?'

'Hardly *ordinary*. You still had that air of good breeding, that finishing-school gloss, and Ashleigh Kent, the firm you worked for, was an up-market one, dealing mainly with wealthy clients wanting country estates and the like. In fact that was where I met you—when I was over in England on a business trip.'

'And you blame me for hooking you?' That explained at least *some* of the hostility she sensed in him.

To her amazement, he shook his head. 'No, I don't blame you for that. It would be different if you'd used your wiles to try and captivate me, but you didn't, did you?'

'I don't know,' she admitted huskily. 'I don't know what I did, how I acted...'

'Like a perfect lady.' His lips twisted into a smile that wasn't a smile. 'You intrigued me from the first moment I laid eyes on you. Though you were obviously attracted to me, you looked at me with such composure, such cool reserve.'

Whereas a lot of women, she guessed, would drool over a man with his kind of looks and that amount of blatant sex appeal.

Slowly, she said, 'You seem pretty sure I was looking for a rich husband...so if I didn't, as you put it, use my "wiles" to try to catch you...' She hesitated. 'Why *didn't* I?'

'When I first asked you to have dinner with me, you refused without giving a reason. I found out later that you already had Graham Ashleigh—who was worth quite a bit—in your sights.

'Though I didn't think the...shall we say attachment...on your side, at least, was too serious, and I had a great deal more to offer financially, it still took me over a week to persuade you to go out with me.'

He sounded annoyed.

Her smile ironic, she suggested, 'Perhaps I was just playing hard to get.'

Privately she thought it far more probable that she'd been chicken—scared stiff by all that overpowering masculinity.

He shook his head. 'Somehow I feel that playing hard to get isn't your style... It certainly wasn't your mother's.'

She flinched at his deliberate unkindness.

'But that's enough delving into the past for the moment,' Jos said decidedly. With a short, sharp sigh, he rose to his feet and stretched long limbs. 'Now I suggest a breath of air. If you have no objection to New Yorkers *en masse*, Saturday afternoon is a good time to take a stroll in the park. Feel up to it?'

His tone was neutral, neither friendly nor unfriendly, and, only too happy to leave the confines of the bedroom, she agreed eagerly. 'Yes, I'd like that.' Then, unwilling to get out of bed while he was there, she added, 'If you'll give me a few minutes...?'

His smile sardonic, he said, 'I'll use the dressing room to change.'

As soon as the door closed behind him, Clare got out of bed and made for the sumptuous bathroom. Whether it was due to the food or to the prolonged sleep, she was pleased to find that the worst of the weakness had gone and she felt much better.

After cleaning her teeth and taking a quick shower, she donned a terrycloth robe while she looked for some fresh undies and something to wear.

A look at the clothes hanging in the walk-in wardrobe suggested that her tastes were quiet and classical rather than flamboyant. For which she was truly thankful.

Trying to rid herself of the feeling that she was rifling another woman's things, she took out a grey and white patterned dress, a white jacket and a pair of high-heeled sandals. Rather to her surprise, everything fitted her perfectly.

When she was dressed she brushed the tangles from her shoulder-length hair. Seeming to be naturally curly, it settled in a soft, dark cloud around her face.

Wrinkling her nose in the mirror at the bruise on her temple, she looked for some tinted foundation to mask it. There was a range of light cosmetics in a pretty, daisy-strewn bag—cream, cleansing lotion and lip-gloss. No sign of any foundation or mascara. Perhaps with dark brows and lashes and a clear skin she didn't use any?

In a side pocket of the bag she came across a narrow flat packet, and froze. Each pill was packed separately and marked with a day of the week.

But that didn't necessarily mean she was like her mother, she told herself firmly. After all, she was a married woman—even if she didn't feel like one...

Hiding her nervousness, her uncertainty, beneath a veneer of calm, she squared her shoulders and went to find Jos.

Everything was quiet and in perfect order. Too perfect. It struck her that the penthouse, with its impersonal opulence, was more like a luxury film-set than a home.

Without her knowing why, the thought made her sad.

In the living room, the long glass panels had been slid aside and he was standing on the terrace looking out across the green leafiness of Central Park. He'd changed into a lightweight suit, the jacket of which was slung over one shoulder and held by a crooked finger.

Clare could have sworn she had made no sound on the thick pale carpet, but, as though some sixth sense was at work, he turned to face her.

Though she didn't *know* him, he was no longer a stranger. Outwardly, at least, he was achingly familiar, and she could have picked him out unerringly from a thousand other tall, dark men.

His hair, brushed straight back from a high forehead, formed a widow's peak, his skin was tanned and his eyes were a clear, brilliant green between thick lashes. He looked tough and intelligent and heart-stoppingly handsome, with the kind of animal magnetism that would have made even an ugly man completely irresistible.

At her approach he held out his hand.

As if under a spell, she put hers into it.

He used the hand he was holding to draw her close, and, smiling into her eyes, bent his head.

Her nostrils were filled with the faint, masculine scent of his aftershave, and, feeling his warm breath on her cheek, she trembled inside while, eyes closed, lips parted, she waited transfixed for his kiss.

But the kiss never came.

When she lifted heavy lids he had drawn back. He was still smiling, but his smile was mocking, derisive.

She didn't need that smile to tell her he was amused by her reaction. Feeling as though she had been slapped in the face, she snatched her hand free and turned away.

Why was he playing with her like this? To remind her that he could? To put her at a disadvantage? For his own entertainment? Or a combination of all three?

Chilled and alarmed, she began dimly to realise something of the power he had over her.

But until her memory returned, and she knew exactly how things stood between them, all she could do was stay calm and resist his potent attraction.

He put on his jacket and, a hand at her waist, accompanied her across the hall and into the lift. Though she was tall and wearing high heels, standing by her side he still seemed to tower over her.

Glancing down at her set profile, he remarked blandly, 'You're looking rather...militant. Something to do with a need for self-preservation?'

She studied his face with calm deliberation, then said, just as blandly, 'And you're looking rather conceited. Something to do with a mistaken belief in your own powers of attraction?'

To her surprise he laughed, and said appreciatively, 'You're starting to sound less like some forlorn waif and more like yourself.'

A moment later the lift slid to a halt and they emerged into the glittering foyer, now thronging with people.

His hand beneath her elbow, he escorted her through the main doors and out onto Fifth Avenue. That famous street was teeming with life and vitality, and had, Clare thought, an air of being *en fête*.

The early evening was hot and sunny, and the park was full of people. Bright summer dresses and colourful umbrellas blossomed everywhere; candy wrappers and soft drink cans littered the paths, radios blared, babies bawled, children played and perspiring joggers jogged.

It was a scene full of noise and gaiety, and Clare loved it.

Jos tucked her hand through his arm and, as he matched his pace to her slower one, they strolled in silence.

After a while, her thoughts busy, she remarked, 'You mentioned we met when you came over to England on a business trip. How did we get to know each other?'

Face guarded, green eyes suddenly wary, Jos answered, 'I'd approached Ashleigh Kent with the intention of buying a house…'

She frowned. Why would he want a house in rural England when he lived in New York?

'You were the representative they sent to show me around.'

A chill feathering over her skin, Clare stopped walking and stood stock-still. As a dim crystal ball, her mind produced a faint, intangible impression of a bare hall, open to the rafters, with dark galleries running round three sides, and a man standing looking up to a pair of high, narrow windows which threw lozenges of light onto the dusty stone flags three floors below.

Head bent, slim fingers pressed to her temples, she tried to seize the elusive memory that hovered almost within her grasp.

Just when she thought she had it, it vanished like a spectre. Suddenly convinced it held some terrible significance, she gave a low moan and began to tremble violently.

Jos took her shoulders. 'Clare, what is it? What have you remembered?'

'Nothing. I…I thought I had, but then it was gone.'

CHAPTER THREE

She was shaking so much that she could scarcely stand. Steering her to the nearest vacant bench, he pushed her onto it and stood over her. After a while the trembling stopped. Gathering herself, she looked up at him and said steadily, 'I'm all right now. We can go on.'

'I think not. You've done enough walking for today. Wait here a moment.'

He went a hundred yards or so to an intersection, where the path they were on was crossed by a wider one. Raising his hand, he snapped his fingers.

As he came back to offer his arm she heard the clatter of a horse's hooves, and by the time they'd reached the intersection a polished black carriage with a top-hatted driver was waiting. It had a festive, holiday air—the well-groomed horse wore yellow rosettes and the driver's whip was adorned with a matching bow of ribbon.

Jos helped her step up and then sat beside her. The driver clicked his tongue at the horse and they were off, bowling merrily through the park.

Clare looked at her companion with awe. 'And I didn't catch a glimpse of either the mouse or the pumpkin.'

He laughed, white teeth gleaming, charm momentarily banishing the hardness. 'There are plenty of these carriages about. The only magic is in knowing where to find an empty one.'

The word 'empty' reminded her of the memory she had so nearly grasped. 'The house I took you to see, was it—?'

'No more questions for the moment,' he broke in firmly. 'Just relax and enjoy the drive. Don't make any attempt to remember. Later on we'll try a spot of therapy, but I was planning to have a meal out first, if you feel up to it?'

So that was why he'd changed into a suit and tie.

'Oh, yes, that would be nice,' she agreed.

The sun shone and, despite the traffic fumes, the balmy evening air fanning her face felt fresh and clean. As they clip-clopped along Jos pointed out all the things of interest, and after a while Clare found herself enjoying the leisurely drive.

It was well past seven when they crossed the Grand Army Plaza and their carriage stopped alongside some others. Beyond rose the pale marble and glazed brick, the richly ornamented mansard of the Plaza Hotel.

'I thought we'd have dinner here tonight,' Jos told her as he helped her down and paid the driver. 'Tomorrow evening, if you like, we can go further afield.'

When he'd given her a glimpse of the celebrated hotel, with its fine shops, lounges and places to eat, he asked, 'Which of the restaurants do you prefer, Clare?'

'I really don't mind. I'll leave it to you.'

'In that case…' With a firm hand beneath her elbow, he steered her towards the nearest, where he appeared to be well known—the maitre d' calling him by name and ushering them to a secluded table for two.

The very air breathed luxury—the rich aroma of smoked salmon and caviare mingling with expensive perfumes and the sweet smell of success. Above the discreet murmur of conversation and an occasional laugh, ice buckets rattled and champagne corks popped.

As they sipped an aperitif and studied the menu Jos made light conversation, giving Clare an opportunity to respond in kind.

She asked him what it was really like to live in Manhattan, and discovered that he was a born raconteur with a pithy way of expressing himself and a dry sense of humour.

'A taxi had just dropped me at Madison and Sixty-third one evening,' he told her, 'when footsteps hurried up behind me and a tough-looking character grabbed hold of my arm. He was picking himself up from the sidewalk for the second time before he managed to explain that I'd lost my wallet and he was trying to return it. To add to my chagrin, when we had a drink together I discovered he was a fellow colleague in the banking business.'

'Is New York a very violent city?' she asked, when she'd stopped laughing.

'There's not as much violence as the media might lead you to believe. Though, as with most big cities, it has its share.'

The food and wine proved to be excellent, and the service first class, but it was the atmosphere that Clare found herself enjoying most, and she said so.

He nodded agreement. 'That's why I come here.'

'Do we tend to like the same things?'

With a strange note in his voice, he said, 'Oh, yes. Though we *can* disagree and have stimulating arguments, it's been clear from the start that our tastes and minds mesh...'

For a moment she felt warmed, though common sense told her that as they didn't love each other there had to have been something, apart from sex, to draw them together.

'For one thing we both enjoy the good life and being rich.'

There was a bitter cynicism in his tone that chilled the warmth, and she recalled his certainty that she'd married him for what he could give her.

'Who wouldn't enjoy being rich?' she asked wryly. 'Though I doubt very much if money can buy real happiness.'

His brilliant gaze on her face, he enquired silkily, 'Still, it must have its compensations? You were prepared to sell yourself...'

'I've only your word that I did.'

'Don't doubt it.'

'But, J—' She broke off, biting her lip, somehow unable to call him by his name.

He reached across the table and took her hand, his thumb pressing menacingly against the soft palm.

'Did I forget to tell you what I'm called?'

'Wh-what?' she stammered.

The green eyes pinned her. 'Do you know what my name is?'

'Of course I know what your name is.'

'You seem unwilling to use it.'

She found herself scoffing, 'Why on earth should I be?'

'Then let me hear you say it.'

Reluctantly, and scarcely above a whisper, she said, 'Jos.'

'Again.'

When she hesitated, he lifted her hand to his lips, biting the fleshy mound at the base of her thumb.

'Jos, please...'

His smile was sardonic. 'That sounded more as if you meant it.'

That little show of dominance effectively spoiled the

calm of the evening, and though he went on to prove himself an entertaining companion she was unable to relax.

They were sipping their coffee when, despite her long sleep, she found herself drooping, having to make an effort to sit up straight.

He noticed at once. 'Getting tired?'

'A little,' she admitted.

He signalled for the bill.

Outside, the summer evening was clear and warm, making the prospect of a short walk back to the Ventnor Building a not unpleasant one. As they began to stroll Jos took her hand.

She shivered, and it had absolutely nothing to do with the little night breeze that had sprung up.

The scent of flowering shrubs drifted across from Central Park, perfuming the air, and far above Fifth Avenue and the lights of the city stars shone in a deep blue sky.

But Clare scarcely noticed the beauty of the night. Tense and *aware*, with her hand imprisoned in his, their arms occasionally brushing, all her attention was focused on Jos.

When they got back to the penthouse though the lights were on there wasn't a sound, and the place appeared to be empty.

Confirming that, Jos remarked casually, 'It's Roberts' night off.'

The realisation that they were quite alone made her feel distinctly apprehensive.

He slid aside the glass panels and led her onto the lamplit terrace to look over the glittering panorama that was Manhattan by night.

As they approached the balustrade she held back.

Feeling her instinctive reluctance, he stopped. 'Have you always been scared of heights?'

'I'm not sure...I don't think so.' She wrinkled her smooth forehead. 'Maybe something happened that frightened me...' As she spoke her skin chilled and a shudder ran through her.

'What is it?' he demanded sharply. 'What do you know?'

'It's nothing... Just someone walking over my grave.' She tried to speak lightly. 'And all I know is, I feel safer back here.'

She was wearing her jacket draped around her shoulders, and as Jos slipped it off he brushed aside the dark silky cloud of hair and kissed her nape.

Feeling that frisson of fear and excitement she experienced every time he touched her, she caught her breath in an audible gasp.

Indicating a luxuriously cushioned swing-seat beyond the splashing fountain, he suggested blandly, 'Why don't you sit down and relax while I get us a nightcap?'

More than uneasy, with all her doubts and worries, her fear of both the future and the past suddenly crowding in on her, she shook her head. 'I think I'll go straight to bed.'

When he said nothing, she added awkwardly, 'Goodnight...Jos.'

She was turning away when his hand shot out and grasped her wrist, bringing her to a halt, not hurting—not if she stood quietly—but keeping her where he wanted her. 'We haven't tried that therapy I mentioned.'

'Therapy?' she echoed unsteadily. 'What kind of therapy?'

'The kind that might help you to remember just what it's like between us.'

Recalling his apparent reluctance to answer some of

her questions, and her own sneaking suspicion that perhaps he didn't *want* her to regain her memory, she was surprised.

Seeing that surprise, he smiled mirthlessly. 'Did you think I'd prefer you *not* to remember?'

'I wondered,' she admitted.

Green eyes gleaming beneath dark, well-marked brows, he shook his head. 'If you didn't get your memory back it would spoil my plans...'

That veiled statement seemed almost to hold a hint of menace, and she was about to ask him what he meant when he went on, 'However, as your remembering might prove to be a two-edged sword, until you're more able to cope I think we should take it easy and not try to hurry things. Except in one area...'

He used the wrist he was holding to draw her closer, so his other hand could raise her chin. His face was only inches away—a lean, attractive face, with beautiful hollows beneath the cheekbones and a mouth that gave her goosebumps.

She felt his breath on her cheek and shivered, her lips suddenly yearning for his. As though he knew, he bent his dark head to touch his mouth to hers.

Last time his kiss had been hard and punishing. This time it was light as thistledown, coaxing and tantalising until her lips parted for him. Then he deepened the kiss, cradling her face between his hands while his mouth made an uncompromising demand that sent her head spinning.

Somehow she knew that she was normally cool and in control, but this man had the power to heat her blood and arouse a fierce, almost overwhelming desire.

He kissed her skilfully, knowledgeably, with a kind of leashed passion that made every nerve-ending zing into life. While he kissed her one hand slid to her nape and the other deftly dealt with the buttons of her dress and the front clip of her dainty bra.

Then his fingers were moving in a tactile exploration, discovering and lingering on the hammering pulse at the base of her throat, stroking across her smooth collarbone, cupping the warm, satiny curve of her breast.

She shuddered as his thumb found and teased the sensitive nipple, sending the most exquisite sensations running through her, making her muscles clench and a core of molten heat form in the pit of her stomach.

He knew exactly what he was doing to her, how to use his mouth and hands to heighten her pleasure and drive her slowly mad, and she was almost lost in a sensual maze of need and hunger when somewhere at the back of her mind a warning bell clanged and she stiffened. If she didn't stop him now, in a very short while she would be unable to.

A part of her protested. Did she *want* to stop him? He *was* her husband...

But a husband she didn't really know.

Using will-power as a whip, she mentally distanced herself. She might have lost her memory but she still had instincts, and every one of those instincts warned her that something was terribly wrong somewhere. If she slept with him now she would be committing herself before she knew what that something was.

Aware of her withdrawal, he stilled his hand and lifted his head to study her flushed face from beneath half-closed lids.

Despite its delicate bone structure, its poignancy, it held no sign of weakness. Indeed, her chin proclaimed a quiet strength, even a hint of stubbornness, and, though passionate, her mouth was set in lines of self-discipline.

Opening heavy lids, Clare saw that the green eyes fixed on her held no warmth or tenderness—no passion, even—only a kind of determination to probe beneath the surface and assess her defences, as if she was an enemy whose strengths and weaknesses he needed to know and calculate.

She hated that cold, impersonal inspection. It told her that whereas his lovemaking had reduced her to a quivering mass of wants and desires, he had been virtually unmoved, his own feelings held in check while with cool expertise he'd aroused hers.

But though he obviously cared little for her, he was her husband and a red-blooded male, and if she'd proved willing he would certainly have taken her to bed.

No doubt he still would.

The thought galvanised her into action. Drawing back abruptly, she caught at the edges of her gaping dress and dragged them together. Then, striving to sound calm, self-possessed, she said, 'I'm afraid your "therapy" hasn't produced any results.'

Seeing the rapid rise and fall of her breasts, and hearing the harshness of her quickened breathing, he observed with ironic amusement, 'Oh, I wouldn't say that. If we were to carry it a little further...'

'No!' Her alarm was evident.

Lifting his shoulders in a slight shrug, he accepted her decision. 'Very well. We'll just have to see what tomorrow brings.'

He wasn't making any attempt to push it—indeed, he was behaving in a thoroughly civilised way—but a hint of something primitive and dangerous hidden beneath his suave manner made her more than wary.

As if to add weight to that impression, he added, 'But bear in mind that you *are* my wife, and I don't intend to go on sleeping in the guest room.'

When he took a step towards her she caught her breath. But, holding her eyes, a cool challenge in his that dared her to protest, he reclipped her bra and fastened the buttons on her dress.

It was *she* who had called a halt, but *he* was very much in command of the situation—as he would be of any situation, she thought bleakly. And, though he was allowing her a free choice at the moment, he'd made it abundantly clear that this state of affairs would only last as long as he permitted it to.

Had his sexual arrogance, his masterfulness, become anathema to her? Was that one of the reasons she had attempted to leave him?

No, surely not. She must have realised what kind of man she was marrying, must have preferred a strong, virile partner to a wimp.

As most women would.

Turning away to stare across the dark trees to the art deco towers of Central Park West, she sighed. He was so blatantly, excitingly *male* that there would have been plenty of willing, not to say eager females flocking round. Small wonder he knew so well how to pleasure a woman...

Contemplating her profile, he offered, 'A penny for them...'

Without stopping to think, she admitted, 'You seem to have a great deal of experience...I was wondering how many women you've loved.'

His dark face sardonic, he said, 'If you're talking about *loved* then the answer's none. Nor have any loved me. I gave up wanting or expecting love a long time ago. But if you mean how many have I gone to bed with, I'm afraid I don't make notches on the bedpost. However, I'm more than willing to refresh your memory on how experienced I am...'

His words caused a convulsive clutch of desire deep in her stomach.

Shaking her head, praying he would take no for an answer, she wondered how long she could hold out against him, and tried to recall if this fierce attraction had been there from the start.

Some instinctive knowledge told her it had sprung into life at their first meeting.

But she had no idea how long ago that was.

Taking a deep breath, she asked jerkily, 'You said we met when you were in England looking for a house...when was that?'

Face guarded, green eyes suddenly wary, Jos answered evasively, 'A few months ago.'

So they couldn't have been married for very long.

It seemed strange to think that with a new husband such as he she couldn't remember what it was like to sleep with him.

But she could imagine the things his lean, skilful hands would do to her, could imagine his weight and the driving force of his body...

Her cheeks growing hot at her own erotic thoughts, she looked hurriedly away from those hard, too perceptive eyes.

'Something bothering you?' he asked blandly.

Schooling her face into a careful blankness, she turned and said, 'I was just wondering how long we've been married.'

Though his lazy, slightly mocking expression didn't alter, she got the distinct impression that it was a question he'd been waiting for. A question he didn't particularly want to answer.

After the briefest pause, he said casually, 'Only a short time.'

'How short?'

He was watching her, eyes gleaming between half-closed lids. 'We were married two days ago.'

'*Two days ago?*' she repeated, startled. 'Then we're...'

'On our honeymoon,' he finished for her. 'So you can understand why I don't find the guest room to my taste.'

Heat running through her, she queried, 'Where were we married? Not here in New York?'

'No, in England. Meredith, to be precise.'

That explained the snapshots.

But if they'd only been married on Thursday, unless they had been lovers previously, they'd spent just one night together. If that...

Unable to ask directly, she said, 'Did we spend our...our wedding night travelling?'

His mocking expression told her he knew what she was getting at, but he answered her question with great exactness. 'No, we spent it here. After a morning wedding and a noon reception we drove to Gatwick and caught an early evening flight to JFK. Because of the time difference we were here at the penthouse by ten o'clock, our time.'

So the marriage had almost certainly been consummated, and she didn't for a moment doubt that he had been a fantastic lover, able to wring the most rapturous responses from her... Yet the very next morning she'd taken off her rings and bolted. Why? *Why?*

'Jos, won't you tell me what happened?'

He raised a dark brow. 'If you want a blow by blow account of our wedding night, it would be easier and much more fun to take up my offer and let me *show* you.'

Hot-cheeked, flustered by his open mockery, she nevertheless stuck to her guns. 'I mean what happened next morning? What did we quarrel about?'

Harshly, he told her, 'I've already said I can't see

much point in discussing it, and that still stands. It was merely a dispute that got out of hand.'

She was almost certain that he was lying.

Surely, in the circumstances, no mere falling out would have made her act that way? Their disagreement must have been over something pretty traumatic.

Something he had no intention of talking about.

She recalled his earlier words, 'your remembering might be a two-edged sword', and guessed that his feelings about it were ambivalent.

Though he'd said it would spoil his plans if she *didn't* remember, she had the strangest notion that he was scared of what it might do to her if she *did*.

So where did that leave them?

As though reading all her doubts and uncertainties, he went on more mildly, 'Look, after a few days in New York we were intending to go upstate. You'd expressed a desire to see Niagara Falls, and we have a suite booked at the Lakeside International on Lake Ontario. If we carry on with our honeymoon as planned—'

'No, I…I *can't*…' she cried in panic.

Controlling his obvious annoyance and frustration admirably, he suggested, 'Suppose we go on *your* terms.'

'You mean…?'

'I mean I'll sleep in the dressing room until you want me in your bed.'

'You won't try to pressure me?'

Grimacing at her caution, he said trenchantly, 'I promise I won't *force* you.'

It wasn't quite the same thing, but after a moment's hesitation she took a deep breath and agreed, 'All right.'

'Then tomorrow morning we'll head for Buffalo.' He took her face between his palms. 'And I suggest that for the next couple of weeks you make a real effort to relax.

Don't keep worrying about the past. Give your memory a chance to come back of its own accord. OK?'

'OK.'

'Good girl.' He smiled and dropped a light kiss on her lips.

Almost more scared of his charm than his anger, she pulled away and fled.

They flew into Buffalo International Airport to find the rental car Jos had ordered waiting for them.

As they began their relatively short drive up to Lake Ontario the weather was clear and bright. Leaving the urban sprawl behind them, they drove with the car windows down, the sun warm on their arms and the breeze ruffling their hair.

Clare discovered that round the great lake was apple country, with mile upon mile of orchards.

'I'm afraid we're too late for the blossom,' Jos remarked, 'and too early for the fruit. But if you come in autumn I'll bet you'll never smell or taste anything more delicious than an Ida Red straight from the tree...'

As its name suggested, the Lakeside International, a quiet, exclusive hotel, was right on the shores of the lake. It was set in well-kept grounds which led down to a private stretch of sand bright with sun-loungers and huge beach umbrellas.

They were greeted by the manager himself, a grey-haired dapper man with a carnation in his buttonhole, and while Jos signed the register a uniformed bellhop hurried to bring their luggage from the car.

Their corner suite was on the ground floor, the green and gold decor throughout giving it an air of cool graciousness.

It had a sumptuous bedroom, with a king-sized canopied bed, an enormous *en suite* bathroom complete with a jacuzzi, and an elegant sitting room furnished with handsome period pieces.

From both the main rooms long French windows opened onto a paved terrace with a lovely view over the garden to the lake. There were several bowls of flowers scattered about, a basket of fresh fruit and a bottle of champagne waiting in an ice bucket.

The only thing it lacked was a dressing room.

Clare's eyes flew to her husband's face and she waited for him to ask to be moved, but, having thanked the bellhop and tipped him generously, he let him go.

As the door closed behind the youth she burst out, 'If you think for one moment...'

The cold blaze in his eyes made the words tail off. His voice brittle, he said, 'I'm sorry there's no dressing room, but, having booked the honeymoon suite in good faith, I don't intend to look a fool by asking to change now.'

Her heart in her mouth, she said, 'But you agreed not to pressure me.'

For a moment he looked furious, then the anger and irritation were swiftly masked. Coming up behind her, he folded his arms around her waist and leaned forward to rub his cheek against hers.

Softly, he asked, 'And you'd regard having to share the same bed as my pressuring you?'

Her heart began to race and fire ran through her, making her face grow hot and melting her very bones. Somehow she found her voice and said, 'Yes, I would. And you *promised*...'

'I only promised not to *force* you. And we both know force wouldn't be necessary...'

Frightened by the truth of his words, she played the only card she'd got. 'I should have had more sense than to trust you to keep to our bargain...'

For an instant his grip tightened, then with a sigh he let her go. 'Very well. As I gave my word, I'll sleep on the couch.'

The brocade-covered couch looked short and narrow and none too comfortable.

'I think I'd better take the couch,' she offered quietly.

'Over my dead body!'

Oh, well, it was up to him.

Keeping his darker side well hidden, and being careful not to upset or disturb her, except in what she guessed was a deliberately calculated *physical* way, with a kind of lazy, good-natured charm that was almost irresistible, Jos set himself out to disarm her and make the holiday a period of calm.

True to his word, he made no attempt to pressure her. Each night, having given up on the couch, he threw a pillow down and, without complaint, slept on the living room floor. But for the rest he insisted on a casual intimacy that continually threatened her composure.

For such a cool and in some ways austere man, he was very physical. He seemed to enjoy touching her.

When they walked he either held her hand or tucked her arm through his. If they were sunbathing, he liked to put sun-screen on her back. And when they lay side by side on the beach he often played with a strand of her hair or stroked the smooth, golden skin of her shoulder with a lean finger.

Keeping up the honeymoon image, he'd arranged for meals to be served in their suite, and, after spending the sunny days exploring the countryside, they ate romantic candlelit suppers on the terrace.

But the thing that disturbed her most was his goodnight kiss. Though he kept it light and easy, the touch of his lips invariably sparked all kinds of wild longings within her, and beneath the veneer of calm unconcern she managed to keep in place she felt breathless and aroused, and was forced to battle against a growing hunger.

Only some sixth sense, some prevailing instinct of danger, prevented her from giving in to the heated excitement that made the blood run through her veins like molten lava.

She felt as though she was walking a tightrope across the crater of a seething volcano. If she once lost her balance she would be lost indeed.

By tacit consent neither mentioned the past or her loss of memory, and though at times the hovering darkness would march forward and press in on her, for the most part Clare managed to exist in a kind of limbo that was far from unpleasant.

The weather remained glorious and, apart from an occasional idle hour or two spent sunbathing on the beach, they used every minute to explore the area.

They visited Oswego, at the lake's edge, Watkins Glen, with its car-racing and its vineyards second only to California's, the Finger Lakes, glacial gouges thought to resemble elongated fingers, and Old Fort Niagara, where uniformed volunteers gave a taste of life as it had been in the early seventeen-hundreds.

Jos proved himself to be a good-tempered, stimulating companion, with an effortless ability to make every excursion enjoyable.

The only time the serenity of the holiday was ruffled, was the day they visited the charming little town of Rochester.

They were passing a high class jeweller's and, having noticed Clare glance at her bare wrist on more than one occasion, Jos paused to look in the window.

When she would have kept walking he held her back,

a hand on her elbow. 'It's high time I bought you a wedding present.'

Unwilling to have him buy her anything, she protested, 'I don't need a wedding present.'

'But I want to buy you one.'

Throwing down the gauntlet, he propelled her into the shop and asked to look at some watches.

Having appraised Jos's casual, but clearly expensive clothes, the salesman produced several gold and jewel-encrusted bracelet watches.

Picking up the gauntlet, with barely a glance at them, Clare shook her head.

The next time the selection was slightly less ostentatious but just as pricey.

A cold knot of apprehension forming in the pit of her stomach, she objected, 'Really, I don't need a watch.'

Jos kept his patience admirably. 'Of course you need a watch, and I want to buy you one.'

'I'd rather you didn't,' she said in a tight little voice.

'Darling, I insist...' An icy fury hidden beneath the smiling endearment, he picked up the most expensive watch there and, holding her wrist in a grip that threatened to bruise the delicate bones, fastened it on. 'There, that looks nice.'

As soon as he let her go, she took it off and put it back on the counter. Bolstered by anger, her stubbornness met and matched his. 'Thank you, darling—' she returned his smile while violet eyes met green in a silent clash of wills '—but I don't much care for that one.'

'Then perhaps you'd like to choose?' His voice was smooth as silk, but his eyes warned of the consequences of further rebellion.

Knowing she was committed now—she couldn't make him look a fool by just walking out—she turned to the salesman and said steadily, 'I'd prefer something much simpler.'

Glancing over an array in a glass showcase, she pointed to a neat, relatively inexpensive little watch on a black leather strap. 'Something like that.'

Disappointed, but too good a salesman to show it, the jeweller opened the case and took out the one she'd indicated.

Carrying the war into the enemy's camp, she held out her wrist to Jos and asked, 'Please won't you fasten it for me, darling?'

For a moment she thought he was going to refuse and insist on her having something better, but, his jaw set, he did as she asked.

When she said, 'Yes, that's much more me,' without a word he drew out his wallet to pay for it.

'Shall I put it in a case for you?' the salesman queried politely.

Clare shook her head. 'There's no need, thank you. I'll keep it on.'

Once outside, as though trying to find an outlet for his anger, Jos walked so fast that she had to almost trot to keep up with him.

When they reached the relative quiet of a small park he stopped beneath the shade of a tree. With a swift movement she was unprepared for he pushed her against the smooth trunk, trapping her there.

She started to protest, but his expression had hardened into a merciless mask which effectively frightened her into silence. Looking up at the hard, ruthless lines and planes of his face, the cool blaze in his green eyes, she froze.

He bent his head so that his face was only inches from hers, and demanded with soft violence, 'What the *hell* were you playing at just now?'

CHAPTER FOUR

'I WANTED—' She broke off abruptly as his hand came up to encircle her throat lightly.

'You wanted to make me look a fool.' His fingers began to stroke gently up and down.

She swallowed convulsively. 'If I'd wanted to make you look a fool I'd have walked out of the shop.'

'You managed quite well as it was.' Then in exasperated fury he went on, 'I've a damned good mind to take that cheap thing off your wrist and throw it away.'

'As you like.' She managed to sound indifferent. 'I never wanted you to buy me a watch in the first place.'

She heard the breath hiss through his teeth. At the same instant she became aware of approaching footsteps, and out of the corner of her eye saw an elderly couple walking slowly towards them.

Jos gave no sign that he'd either heard or seen them, but his hand moved to cup her face and his mouth swooped to cover hers.

His kiss seemed to obliterate time and space, to go on for ever. At first it was cold, punitive, a means of venting his anger, then it became heated and hungry, an ardent demand that she was unable to refuse.

When he finally lifted his head, every bone in her body felt as though it had turned to water, and if it hadn't been for the support of the tree she would have slid into a heap.

She opened heavy violet eyes to find he was staring

down at her, and momentarily he looked as dazed by passion as she was.

A second later his face was wiped clear of all emotion and he said thinly, 'Don't ever do anything like that to me again, Clare.'

'I won't if you don't try to buy me any more expensive presents,' she retorted jerkily.

He looked genuinely surprised. Then he smiled sardonically. 'Not wanting to take the perks without coming up with the goods?'

'That aspect hadn't crossed my mind.'

'In that case why the objection to me buying you something?'

'Until I *know* why I married you, I prefer to think it wasn't for your money.'

'Ah… So that hit a nerve, did it? But then truth often does. Don't look so upset. I don't mind.' He smiled mirthlessly. 'Knowing why you married me salves my conscience.'

She was still worrying over the implications of that last remark when he said, 'Look, I don't want to upset what is supposed to be a therapeutic period by quarrelling. It's up to you whether you keep the watch or throw it away.'

In a small voice, she said, 'I'd like to keep it.'

'Very well.' He brushed a strand of dark silky hair away from her cheek. 'And if it's going to upset you, I won't spend money on costly presents, but I reserve the right to buy my wife candy or flowers or any inexpensive gift that takes my fancy.'

'But I've nothing to give you in return.'

His smile was crooked. 'Oh, I wouldn't say that.'

'I don't even know if I've got any money,' she ploughed on desperately.

'I'll give you whatever you need, and as soon as we

get back to New York I have every intention of opening a bank account for you.'

'But that would be *your* money. I couldn't spend that on you.'

'Then just give me a kiss.'

'It would seem as though you were buying my kisses,' she said stiffly.

He sighed with exasperation. 'All right, *don't* give me a kiss. You don't even need to say thanks.'

Suddenly weary of arguing, wanting to defuse the situation and get back on the friendly footing they'd achieved over the past few days, she widened her eyes and said in mock-horror, 'I'm sure that posh finishing-school you once mentioned would be shocked to think I'd learnt no better manners than that.'

His face relaxed into a smile of genuine amusement. With his wide forehead, high cheekbones and straight, bony nose, he had an inordinately handsome face that gave the impression of stark, uncompromising strength. Smiling, he was even more attractive, the harshness overlaid with humour.

'OK, so thank me. Now, come on—' reaching for her hand, he tucked it through his arm '—let's forget the past half-hour and start enjoying ourselves again.' Then he added with a slight bite, 'And just so you don't get uptight about what I'm spending on you, I'll try to find a cheap café to buy you a coffee.'

After that conversation he made a point of buying her a cheap gift almost every time they went out.

On the first occasion it was a large, cross-eyed teddy bear—so ugly, he said mournfully, that it needed some-one to love it.

'I love it already,' she assured him. Adding serenely, 'But it's a bit cumbersome, so I'm sure you'll carry it back to the car for me.'

After that he stuck to flowers or candy.

On what was to be the last weekend of their honeymoon, Jos was planning to take her to see Niagara Falls. On the Saturday morning, after breakfasting early on the sunny terrace, Clare was feeding crumbs of toast to the sparrows when he surprised her by saying, 'You'll need to pack an overnight bag before we go.'

'I thought we weren't very far away.'

'We're not. But when we first discussed our honeymoon you expressed a desire to stay near the falls. I wasn't keen. Hotels there can be noisy and crowded... However, so you won't miss out totally, I've managed to book at the Luna Towers for tonight and tomorrow night.'

Having gathered from various tourist brochures that the Luna Towers had one of the most spectacular views of the falls, Clare exclaimed, 'Oh, thank you! How nice of you.'

To her surprise he looked disconcerted, a faint wash of colour appearing along his hard cheekbones. Curtly, he said, 'You'd better save your eulogies until I tell you that the best I could manage was one double room.' As she took in the implications of that, he added, 'Of course, if you'd rather, we could always come back here.'

Knowing what trouble he must have gone to to secure even one room at the Luna Towers at the height of the season and at such short notice, she shook her head. 'I'd like to stay at the falls.'

But what if the room had a double bed? She could hardly expect him to go on sleeping on the floor...

That thought was followed by an even more disturbing one.

Suppose Jos was banking on that very thing? He'd

been extremely patient, but what if he'd decided to take this opportunity to strip off the kid gloves?

Watching her expressive face, he asked sardonically, 'Changed your mind?'

Lifting her chin, she met the challenge of his brilliant gaze, and, though all manner of warning bells were sounding, said calmly, 'No, I haven't changed my mind.'

After a good run through to Niagara they checked in at the busy hotel, and then, having been provided with a picnic lunch, left the car there and set off on foot to take a closer look at the falls.

Their stroll took them through a pleasant, lightly wooded area, which was alive both with tourists and squirrels.

The fact that their large, comfortable room was furnished with twin beds had done a lot to ease Clare's worries, and she walked with a little smile on her lips, prompting Jos to remark sardonically, 'You look happy...or should I say relieved?'

Flushing a little, she said mendaciously, 'I was just thinking how tame the squirrels are.'

'They're used to being fed.'

As though to prove his point, a black squirrel made a short rush and stopped right in their path, his plume of a tail arched over his back, pointed ears pricked, bright eyes hopeful.

'Oh, isn't he sweet?' she exclaimed. 'I don't think I've ever seen a black one before... Oh, I'm sorry I've nothing suitable to give you.'

Feeling in the brown paper carrier bag that held their lunch, Jos produced a bag of nuts. 'Try one of these.' Smiling at her astonishment, he said, 'I asked for them specially. You have a penchant for feeding things. In Meredith it was the ducks.'

Opening the bag, she asked, 'But how did you know about the squirrels?'

'I've been here before.'

When she crouched down, the animal took the proffered nut from her fingers, and in the twinkling of an eye they were surrounded by a dozen or more of the appealing rodents, who ranged in colour from pale cream through to chocolate and jet-black.

As soon as the last of the nuts had been distributed Jos put the empty bag into the pocket of his cotton jacket, and, while they carried on to the falls, the furry gang went off to mug the next willing tourist.

Clare could hear the thunder of the falls well before they reached them, and felt a growing excitement. Up close, she found the smooth rush of water plummeting over the edge disorienting, and instinctively reached for Jos's hand.

It closed around hers and squeezed, the warmth of the little gesture making her heart sing with a sudden gladness. For the first time since waking in hospital she felt optimistic about the future—hopeful that, whether she regained her memory or not, things might turn out well after all.

'So what do you think?' he asked. 'Worth the trip?'

'They're magnificent,' she breathed in awe.

'To get the best view, I suggest that after lunch we walk over Rainbow Bridge to the Canadian side...'

Sitting in the sun by the fast-flowing Niagara, talking companionably, they unpacked their picnic of ham and sourdough bread and fruit.

A bedraggled-looking water bird appeared and watched them with black, shoe-button eyes.

'Poor thing, it looks hungry,' Clare exclaimed, and threw it a chunk of bread.

After studying her for a moment or two, Jos remarked,

'I'm continually surprised by how tender-hearted you've grown up to be.'

'You sound as if you knew me when I was young, and I was a heartless little monster.' Then with a puzzled frown she asked, '*Did* you know me?'

After a split second's hesitation, he said, 'I didn't need to know you. In my experience a lot of children can be heartless little monsters, and usually the females stay that way.'

Which only echoed his poor opinion of women.

She shook her head. 'You're a cynic.'

'I'm a realist. Though I must admit that at times you're so soft-hearted you tend to confound me.' Though he spoke teasingly, there was an underlying current of seriousness.

Having finished her ham sandwich, Clare fished in the carrier and offered him a tin of cola.

He shook his head. 'I must be one of the few people in the States who doesn't like it. Probably because I wasn't brought up with it.'

'What *were* you brought up with? Good old British lemonade?'

'I guess you could say that,' he answered lightly.

Passing him a peach, Clare pursued the subject. 'I don't really know anything about you...the names of your parents...where you lived...which school you went to...if you have any brothers or sisters...'

He bit into the peach with care. 'I thought we'd agreed not to worry about the past.'

'*My* past. It can't do any harm to tell me about *yours*.'

Glancing up, Clare saw that all the warmth had vanished from his face, leaving it curiously bleak and empty.

Judging by his expression, his childhood had been anything but happy, and, wishing she'd never asked, she said hurriedly, 'Of course, if you'd rather not talk about it...'

'Why not?' His tone was brittle. 'You'll need to know some time.'

She was just thinking that that seemed an odd way to phrase it, when he went on in a curiously formal way, 'I was the only child of Charles and Rebecca Saunders. We lived in a rural area fairly close to London. The house, our family's home for generations, had belonged to my grandfather, but after my grandmother's death, he couldn't stay. He gave Foxton Priory to my father, and travelled a great deal before eventually reaching the States. After crossing from the eastern seaboard to the west, and making money in various ventures, he went up to Alaska and joined a mining consortium.

'My father was a businessman turned politician. My mother, who adored him, gave up everything to support his political ambitions. She entertained his colleagues and constituents, sat on committees and attended endless charity functions...

'If *you* were a mistake, so was I.' Just for a moment his bitterness was searing. 'I always felt rejected. My father had no time to bother with me, and my mother was too busy taking care of him. Her husband's career and interests came first. Oh, I don't mean to say I was *neglected*—they appeared to be wealthy, able to provide every material thing I could have wished for.

'My mother hired a nanny to take care of me until I could be sent away to boarding-school, but I loved Foxton Priory and didn't want to go. Nanny kept assuring me I was too young at seven, but she was wrong...'

His voice was flat, hard as polished granite. 'You know what they say about hope springing eternal? Well, each time I came home for the school holidays I hoped my mother wouldn't send me back. I told myself that things might alter and improve, that she might have more time for me.

'Finally things did change, but not for the better. I discovered that all my mother's devotion had been for nothing. My parents' marriage was crumbling, on the point of breaking up. My father was embroiled in an affair. I overheard them quarrelling, talking about a divorce...'

'Quite a few of the other boys' parents were separated or divorced, but I'd never thought of it happening to mine.

'In the event it didn't. My mother died and a few weeks later my father was killed when his car careered off the road and hit a tree head-on. It said in all the papers that he was hopelessly drunk at the time.'

Glimpsing the pain and futile anger beneath the dispassionate words, Clare caught her breath.

'My parents' *appearance* of wealth turned out to be just that. The house I loved was mortgaged up to the hilt and there was no money to pay my next term's school fees.'

Without a trace of self-pity, he continued, 'All that was left, the solicitors informed me, was a heap of worthless mining stock that my grandfather, who had died in Alaska the previous year, had left me, and a load of debts. I was thirteen at the time. An awkward age. I had no close relatives, no one who wanted me...'

He was watching her face closely, almost as if he was waiting for some reaction.

Knowing instinctively that it wasn't pity he was looking for, she remained still and silent.

'I was put into council care, then sent to foster-parents. I didn't fit in, and their own son hated me. The boys at school made fun of me, and I was frequently in trouble for fighting.

'My foster-parents did their best to tame me—Mary Kelly with secret bribes, her husband, John, by leathering the daylights out of me. He was a heavily built six-footer, and a bully by nature. I was almost sixteen when he accused me of stealing money out of his pocket to go to the local cinema. Mary had given me the money, and I told him that. But when he asked her, she swore she hadn't...'

No wonder Jos had no liking for women, Clare thought bleakly. Every woman in his life appeared to have failed him in some way.

'It was only later that I realised she was probably too scared to admit it. Anyway, he called me a lying, thieving bastard and laid into me with a strap. By that time I was getting some muscles of my own. I knocked him down and walked out. I never went back.

'With what was left of the money I took a train up to London. I slept rough for a night or two before managing to find a bed in a hostel. After a few days I was lucky enough to get a live-in job in a pub, humping barrels of beer and doing the heavy work. With the money I earned I took a business course and set out to better myself. I found I had a flair for the stock market, and by the time I was twenty, though far from rich, I was making a healthy profit.

'I wanted to make a clean break with the past, so I contacted my father's solicitors, and, with a view to paying off the debts he'd left, arranged to go in to see them.

'There was a surprise waiting for me. They had been advertising, trying to contact me. The "worthless stock" my grandfather had left me had, almost overnight, become worth millions with the Alaskan mining company's discovery of huge deposits of gold.'

So that was the source of his wealth.

Sounding cool and detached, he went on, 'I found that

money breeds money. I bought out a small merchant bank and turned it into a big one, and during the next five or six years acquired property and various businesses that put me securely in the wealthy class.'

Wealth that had come too late to save what must have been years of hell. 'It's a pity the mining company didn't strike lucky sooner,' Clare commented with a sigh.

To her surprise, he shook his head. 'Those years taught me a lot. They taught me to be tough, to be ruthless. Taught me to hate. Taught me that money buys power—'

'But not necessarily happiness,' she broke in swiftly, appalled by such black bitterness.

'It buys what I want,' he told her with savage satisfaction. 'It bought you.'

Bending her head, she looked down, all her new-found hope and optimism dying in the grass at her feet.

He rose, uncoiling his length in one swift movement, and held out his hand. Just for an instant she had the strangest feeling that he was regretting his words, but, his voice curt, all he said was, 'About ready to move?'

She nodded, and, putting her hand into his, let him haul her to her feet.

Unable to look at him, scared he'd see just how badly he'd wounded her, she stopped and began collecting their litter to drop into the nearest bin.

Money didn't make a successful marriage any more than a wedding ring made a happy wife, she thought sadly, as, hand in hand, they set off to walk to Rainbow Bridge. But at least she was coming to understand him a little better and to know something of her own feelings.

What he'd gone through had hardened him, warped him, destroyed his ability to love and trust, made it difficult for him to accept, or even recognise love.

For she had loved him. It hadn't been merely a physical attraction that had drawn her to him. Remembering the snapshot that had been taken on the day they'd got engaged, she *knew* she had loved him. It had been implicit in her look, her smile, her whole bearing.

That was why she'd married him. Not for his money or the lifestyle he could give her, but for the oldest and most bitter-sweet of reasons.

Only he'd never known, and if she told him now he wouldn't believe her... But why hadn't she told him *then*?

Perhaps, aware that he didn't love her, she'd been too proud to. Maybe she had kept silent, hoping she could *show* him she cared, hoping eventually to strike an answering spark. Though surely knowing about his loveless childhood...

But *had* she known? He'd said, 'You'll need to know some time', but had he meant *know* or *remember*?

'Jos...?'

He glanced down at her enquiringly, green eyes gleaming between thick dark lashes.

'Did I know about your childhood? I mean, before I lost my memory.'

His face suddenly inscrutable, he said, 'I'd never mentioned it to you. Why do you ask?'

'I just wondered.'

So, not knowing about his childhood, she wouldn't have been aware of how necessary it was to tell him she cared, to make him believe she loved him. She'd kept it hidden, and in doing so had convinced him that she was marrying him for what he could give her. No wonder he was so bitter and cynical...

Reaching the bridge, mingling with a small throng of sunburnt tourists, they crossed into Canada—Jos producing their passports for Canadian Customs—and followed the crowd along a bustling thoroughfare, with the

Niagara Gorge on one side and the other lined with shops and cafés and amusements.

'Ah, just what we need!' he exclaimed suddenly, and, stopping at a kiosk, proceeded to buy a couple of plastic-hooded yellow capes.

'Expecting rain?' she queried.

He grinned with a flash of white teeth. 'Believe me it pays to wear a mac. Here—' he shook one out '—put it round you.'

A little dubious, she asked, 'Are you sure it's necessary?'

'Unless you want to end up drenched to the skin by spray.'

Before they'd gone more than a hundred yards or so she discovered that Jos had been right. The pavement and the roadway were wet and the air was full of a fine mist.

Some people wore raincoats, one or two carried umbrellas, but quite a few were unprepared. A group of youths swaggered along, getting wet with macho pride, while girls in summer frocks shrieked and giggled as they tried to stay out of range of the blown spray.

When they got to the viewing-point, the roar of the falls and the sheer spectacle took Clare's breath away. She gazed entranced at the never-ending avalanche of water thundering onto the rocks, and the flashing rainbows made by the sun slanting through the spray.

Turning shining eyes on her companion, she exclaimed, 'Aren't they *wonderful*? I heard someone mention the Bridal Veil Falls—which are they?'

'The Bridal Veil Falls are the smallest. Tomorrow, if you'd like to take a closer look, we'll go across the footbridge to Luna Island, where you can get a bird's-eye view... But perhaps the most exhilarating way to see the whole panorama is to take a boat trip on the *Maid of the Mist*...'

'That sounds like fun, but a bit scary.'

'Afraid of being on the water?'

'I don't think so... But there's only one way to find out.'

He saluted her spirit before saying, 'The *Maid* leaves from Prospect Point on the American side, so we'll be nice and handy. But now time's getting on and you must be tired, so I suggest we make our way back to the hotel and have Buffalo Wings for dinner.'

'What on earth are they?'

His grin made him suddenly boyish. 'Wait and see.'

Once back they took it in turns to shower and change—Clare into a silky, blue and mauve evening skirt and matching camisole top fastened with tiny self-buttons, Jos into a white lawn shirt left open at the throat.

They ate the spicy Buffalo Wings, which turned out to be chicken, on their balcony. There was a marvellous view of the falls and the scented air was balmy. In the gathering blue dusk a flock of small birds wheeled about overhead before settling in the trees like black snow.

On the table the candle flame flickered in the faint breeze, casting shadows on Jos's strong face and making his eyes gleam silver.

It couldn't have been a more romantic setting.

Beneath her lashes she watched him move the tip of his tongue across his lower lip and shivered slightly, wanting to follow it with her own tongue. Wanting to touch him.

As if he'd read her mind, he reached across the small table and lifted her hand to his lips. She gave a little gasp as, turning it slightly, he kissed the palm, his tongue tracing the heart line.

The deliberately sensual act turned the violet of her eyes almost to purple, and tore a rent a yard wide in her composure. When he released her hand she hid it in her lap, nursing it as though it was wounded, feeling a sharp pang of regret for what might have been.

Their holiday was almost over and she still hadn't regained her memory, nor did she know what had made her leave him. If only things had been different and this had been a real honeymoon...

But it *was* a real honeymoon. The fact that she had lost her memory didn't make it any less real, only a great deal more difficult.

As difficult as facing the future would be if she didn't get her memory back.

Without her past—her emotions, her awareness, her experience—she was incomplete, like a one-dimensional cardboard cut-out.

No, that made her seem lifeless, without feelings. She was more like a shadow who had lost its substance and was left alone and scared and bewildered.

Though she was sure now that she had married Jos for the right reasons, she was equally sure that he had married her for the wrong ones.

She sighed. There was still so much she didn't understand. Strange undercurrents, nuances she could almost but not quite catch, the way he often seemed to use words to conceal thoughts rather than express them, a feeling that at times he regarded her as an enemy.

And always at the back of her mind that lingering feeling of unease and apprehension, as though subconsciously she knew something dark and deep and terrible that she was unable to bring into the open and face squarely.

Suppose she'd done something awful? Something that

Jos wouldn't tell her. Something, that with very mixed feelings, he was waiting for her to remember.

But what if she never did? She gave another short, sharp sigh.

'I'd like to think those were contented, languorous sighs, but I rather feel they're anxious ones.'

She tried to keep her head bent but his will dragged her glance upwards.

He was watching her, his brilliant eyes boring into her. 'What's wrong, Clare?'

The words came in a rush. 'It's over two weeks now and there's still no sign of my memory coming back. Surely the more days that pass, the less chance there is...?' Agitation bringing her to her feet, she cried hoarsely, 'Suppose I *never* get it back?'

He rose in one swift movement and came round the table to take her upper arms in a firm grip. 'That's a possibility we may have to face. But if there's no *physical* reason, and Dr Hauser assured me there isn't, it's much more likely that you *will* get it back. Though he did stress that pressure of any kind could have adverse effects...that the past should be allowed to come back in its own good time.'

'So what do I do while I'm waiting?' she asked bleakly.

'Just what we have been doing. No effort of will can bring it back, so all we can do is carry on with our lives as if—'

All the tensions that she had managed to ignore for the past fortnight suddenly surfaced like sharks. 'As if I'm normal instead of some kind of freak?'

'Don't be silly, Clare,' he said shortly.

'Well, that's what I feel like. Someone who's only half alive, with no past and no future, on honeymoon with a man I don't remember marrying, a husband who is to all intents and purposes a stranger...'

Just for an instant his fingers bit painfully into her soft flesh, then they released her, and, his smile as slow and premeditated as a striptease, he said, 'Well, tonight I think we should remedy that state of affairs.'

CHAPTER FIVE

SHE caught her breath in shock. 'No, no I won't—'

A single finger touched her lips, effectively cutting off her instinctive protest. 'Oh, but you will, my darling wife,' he told her with icy determination. 'I've waited long enough. Too long. There would have been a lot less tension if I'd made love to you that first night at the International, instead of sleeping on the floor. I held back to give you time to adjust, to get used to the idea of being married to me, but it doesn't seem to have worked.'

'If you mean I still don't want to sleep with you, then you're right.'

'Why this show of reluctance? It's quite out of character.'

She flushed a little. 'Even if I'm the kind of woman you say I am, I'm sure I've always wanted to *choose* who I slept with.'

'I'm your husband. You *chose* to marry me; I didn't force you.'

But she felt oddly convinced that, if necessary, he would have been prepared to.

'So why shouldn't I have what I'm convinced you've dispensed with...shall we say...abundant generosity...?'

Though her heart felt as if it was being squeezed in a giant nutcracker, she fought back. 'Are you sure you're not mixing me up with my mother?'

'I doubt it. Any woman with your looks and sex appeal must have had plenty of propositions.'

'That doesn't mean to say I accepted any of them.'

His laugh was almost a sneer. 'In a minute you'll be trying to tell me you're still a virgin.'

'And you think that's impossible?'

She was waiting for him to say, I *know* it's impossible, but he said, 'I certainly think it's *improbable*. You're nearly twenty-five. There can't be too many twenty-five-year-old virgins about.'

'Especially *married* ones.'

'Ah!' he murmured softly. 'So now you know what you didn't want to ask.'

'And what you didn't want to tell me. *Why* didn't you want to admit that our marriage hadn't been consummated?'

'Because I thought it would make things easier to let you believe that we'd already crossed the Rubicon.'

'Easier for *you!*'

'For both of us.'

Everything he'd said and done pointed to the fact that though he might not love her he certainly *wanted* her, so why hadn't their marriage been consummated?

Smiling a little, once again reading her mind, he drawled, 'I'm more then willing to prove I'm not impotent, if that's what's worrying you…?'

The idea laughable, she half shook her head. At that instant a thought struck her, and she asked sharply, 'How long were we engaged?'

His eyes narrowed a little. 'Six weeks.'

'And we were never lovers…' It was a statement rather than a question. Lifting her head, she met his eyes. 'Why?'

He shrugged. 'You held back.'

She found that difficult to believe.

'Why did I hold back? If I'm as free with my…
er…favours as you seem to think…'

'Perhaps you were making sure of the wedding ring
first. But now you have one—' he picked up her hand
and twisted the broad band of chased gold round her
slim finger '—so the time for excuses and holding back
is over.'

Before she had guessed his intention, he'd stooped
and swept her into his arms. Suddenly unnerved by his
arrogant self-confidence, his undoubted strength, she began to fight.

Holding her easily, despite her struggles, he carried
her inside the room and tossed her onto the nearest bed.

Switching on the bedside lamp, he sat beside her, his
hip touching hers, and, gripping her wrists, pressed her
hands into the pillow, one each side of her head.

Her hair was a dark cloud around her heart-shaped
face, her violet eyes almost black with fear and anger.

'Let me go,' she whispered fiercely. 'I don't want to
sleep with you.'

'You will.' He bent his head until his mouth was only
inches from hers. 'Your breathing has quickened, and
there's a telltale pulse hammering away in your throat.
When I kiss you you'll start to respond, and five minutes
later you'll be begging me to make love to you.'

'Like I did on our wedding night?' she taunted.

'You have a sharp tongue, my darling. But then I like
a little spirit.'

Hating her own defencelessness, she begged, 'Please,
Jos… I don't want to make this marriage a real one—
not until I get my memory back, until I *know* how things
were between us.'

'As I've said before, you *chose* to marry me…'

'But on our wedding night it seems I didn't choose to
sleep with you.'

'All right, so we quarrelled. But there's no call to let your imagination run riot. I didn't suddenly grow horns and a forked tail and turn into the devil himself...'

He was doing his best to play things down, but the instinct that had warned her of danger was still there, sharp and insistent.

'All I'm asking is to wait until I get my memory back,' she pleaded.

'And suppose you never do?' His voice was suddenly harsh. 'You're a passionate woman with needs. What do you intend to do? Sleep with every man who comes along rather than with your own husband? No, Clare, I've been patient long enough.' A set purpose hardened his dark face into ruthlessness. 'If you won't give me what I want, then I'll have to take it.'

He swooped and covered her mouth with his own. It wasn't the brutal assault she was expecting, but a light brush of lips and tongue, a startling sensation made all the more sensual by the lightness, the delicacy of his touch.

She tried to keep her mouth closed against him, but his tongue-tip parted her lips and brushed the sensitive inner skin, making her gasp and quiver. He caught her lower lip between his teeth and began to suck and tug gently.

It was the most erotic thing she had ever experienced, and her stomach clenched and contracted at each pull.

What he was doing to her was so mind-bending that she scarcely noticed that he'd released her wrists and that his fingers were unfastening the buttons of her silky top and the front clip of her bra.

Her nipples were firm, waiting for his touch, and as his mouth followed his teasing fingers she began to make little whimpering sounds deep in her throat, trapped in a web of sensual enchantment.

As though he found her exquisite, and beautiful, he undressed her slowly, carefully, touching and stroking, unerringly finding and stimulating every erogenous zone.

She made no move to escape, lying in a pool of lamplight, helpless, dazed, her mind drugged with sensations so meltingly sweet that she was held in thrall.

Her body was slim yet curvaceous, with firm, beautifully shaped breasts, flaring hips and long, slender legs. Against the thin white sheet her skin was the palest gold, fine and flawless.

When she was naked, he turned her onto her stomach and kissed and caressed a leisurely path from her nape to the soles of her narrow feet, following the bumps and indentations of her spine, smoothing her buttocks, seeking the unexpectedly sensitive skin behind her knees with a warm tongue, making her wriggle and squirm, before turning her onto her back again.

Her breath was coming in quick shallow gasps between parted lips and her eyes were tightly closed, long lashes lying like black fans against her flushed cheeks.

He studied her for a long moment before bending his head to kiss her again. His mouth was gentle, yet with a hint of violence held strictly in check.

This time, at the mercy of sensations she couldn't remember ever experiencing before, she let her lips part helplessly, and he deepened the kiss, exploring her mouth like a conqueror.

When finally he lifted his head she put her arms around his neck, on fire for him, and tried to draw him back to her.

He laughed softly, triumphantly, and pulled away to strip off his own clothes.

In those few seconds of anticipation she knew instinctively how his weight would feel, what shape his body would take as it enclosed hers...

Then he was back, naked flesh against naked flesh, his hard legs parting her soft thighs, his lean hands stroking her breasts, his mouth on hers.

As he drew her down into the heated, erotic depths of passion, mingled with her breathless excitement was a sudden feeling of certainty, of *rightness*. All her doubts and fears belonged to a bad dream. This was reality. She and this tough, complex man belonged together. He was hers. Her husband. Her love...

'Oh!' A sudden tearing pain made her cry out.

She felt him freeze in shock, and, fearing he might be going to pull away and leave her bereft, she said hoarsely, 'It's all right... It's all *right*...' and held him to her, her arms across his broad back.

Still he hesitated, and with an instinct as old as time she pressed the lower half of her body against his and moved her hips enticingly.

With an inarticulate sound he began to move again, slowly, carefully, building up a spiralling core of tension until, passion riding him, he gave a kind of growl and drove hard and fast as she shuddered beneath him in convulsive ecstasy.

When, a second or two later, he groaned her name, she barely heard him, lost in a world of pure sensation. And them, with his head heavy against her breast, she slept.

When she awoke to instant and complete remembrance the room was dark, and cool air wafted softly in from the French windows. Still euphoric, she sighed and stretched like a satisfied cat.

If she'd dreamt it could be like this, she would never have held out against him for an instant, she thought, and turned to look at the other bed.

It was empty.

Feeling a sudden chill that had nothing to do with the

night breeze, she sat up. At the same instant she caught sight of the dark silhouette standing still and silent on the terrace.

Slipping out of bed, she pulled on the satin robe that she'd tossed over a chair earlier and, tying the belt as she went, padded out to him.

Though she guessed he'd heard her coming, he made no move. Not until she touched his arm did he turn his head to look at her.

He might have been looking at a total stranger.

Her heart sank. He'd believed her to be experienced and clearly she wasn't... Perhaps he preferred a more sophisticated woman?

'Jos...? What's wrong?'

'What should be wrong?' he asked shortly.

She bit her lip, then persevered, '*Something* is. Did I...? I mean, were you...disappointed?'

'Because you were a virgin?'

There was such bitterness in his voice that she found herself stammering, 'I—I'm sorry...'

'What in heaven's name are you apologising for?' he burst out.

'You sounded as if you thought I was to blame for misleading you.'

'No, I'm the one to blame.' He turned away, his hands gripping the balustrade until his knuckles gleamed white. 'Before we got married we discussed contraception—I knew you were already taking the pill.'

'Yes, I found them. But some women take them for other reasons...'

As though she hadn't spoken, he went on, 'And because you *look* like your mother, without any concrete proof I somehow convinced myself that you must *be* like her.'

Every time he mentioned her mother his voice held

the same sharp edge of contempt and animosity that conveyed much more than mere disapproval…

The thought crystallising, Clare said slowly, 'You *hated* her.'

He didn't answer. But then he didn't need to.

She wanted to ask him why, how he could hate a woman he hadn't even known. But an instinctive feeling that this wasn't the time or place held her back. And there were more important considerations—things she needed to know now she had committed herself.

Taking a deep breath, she broke the tense silence to ask, 'The fact that I'm not experienced…does it make any difference?'

'In what respect?'

'Well, if you'd prefer a woman who knows how to please you…' She faltered into silence.

'I won't be looking elsewhere, if that's what you're thinking. One woman is all I need. And, contrary to what you seem to imagine, I haven't had endless affairs. In fact I'm rather fastidious in my choice of lovers. When no one matches up to what I'm looking for, I've even been known to be celibate for months at a time.'

Though she felt halfway towards being reassured, it wasn't precisely what she'd been asking. Gathering her courage, she said, 'I meant would you have married me if you'd known?'

'Oh, yes.' His voice was pure polished steel. 'Though at first I was thrown, it doesn't really alter anything…'

Without knowing why, she shivered.

'In some ways it makes things easier. Now I can teach you everything I want you to know, and you'll be mine in a way I never expected you to be.'

He turned and took her chin, lifting her face to his. It was too dark to read his expression but his desire beat against her like black wings.

When he led her back into the bedroom she went with undisguised eagerness, not to say abandon, breathless and trembling a little.

Jos made love to her again, and this time there was no pain, only a wild explosion of excitement and delight, and while she lay with her head on his shoulder she felt a gradual slide into a warm sea of mindless oblivion.

When she awoke it was to daylight and to shuddering sensation. He'd pushed the sheet away and his lips and tongue were travelling over her stomach, making a sensuous exploration of the warm flesh he'd laid bare.

As his mouth moved lover she gasped, 'No, Jos,' and made an instinctive attempt to reject such intimacy. His hands tightened on her thighs, his fingers biting painfully.

'You're hurting me,' she protested.

He lifted his head and she saw the hard, clear-cut lines and planes of his face, the blaze in his green eyes, the arrogance.

'Then lie still.'

A moment later his mouth was warm against her flesh again and his tongue was flicking and probing, insisting that she yield to the erotic pleasure he was giving her.

Only when she gave a little cry and arched towards him did he release his grip and cover her body with his own. 'Now relax. I'm going to show you the difference in sensations, make love to you until I've made you feel what it's like to...' His lips brushing her ear, he whispered his intentions.

'I *can't*...' she breathed.

He laughed softly. 'Of course you can. A twenty-five-year-old virgin bride has a lot of catching up to do.'

But she couldn't *stand* any more, she thought a shade wildly, before all thought was washed away and sensation after sensation began to flood through her body in slow waves of pleasure and delight...

After they'd showered and eaten a late breakfast on the balcony, his green eyes gleaming, Jos queried, 'Do you want to go out?'

She had begun to shake her head when, wondering if even his magnificent virility was starting to flag, she said hastily, 'Unless you do?'

Laughing under his breath, he hung a 'Do not disturb' notice on the door, and they went back to share the single bed.

Jos made no attempt to hide his satisfaction at the way things had turned out, and when they returned to the Lakeside International he made arrangements to stay on for a further week.

Having bulldozed down the barriers, he proved to be an exciting, inventive lover, with what a blushing Clare told him was an almost insatiable appetite.

He only laughed, and with consummate skill proceeded to prove that he could make her just as hungry for him.

She might have been a virgin, but he seemed to have tapped a latent spring of desire and need, and she was startled and somewhat alarmed to realise what a warm, sensual woman had been lying hidden beneath the cool surface.

So much so that she wondered how she had managed to remain a virgin for so long. Unless, scared by her mother's excesses, her own passionate nature had been deliberately suppressed?

Perhaps that was why she had been able to hold out against Jos? That and the uncomfortable knowledge that he hadn't loved her.

And he still didn't, she admitted sadly. He didn't even *like* her.

There was no doubt that he *desired* her, but his coolness was only melted by the heat of passion, never by the gentle warmth of affection. And though he gave free rein to his passion, her suspicion that he regarded his need for her as a weakness, and despised himself accordingly, added an extra and disturbing dimension to an already fraught relationship.

Each time she lay in his arms she hoped that things would change, that one day he would look at her with tenderness in his eyes. But always she was conscious of a fundamental hostility, usually carefully hidden, but present nevertheless.

Neither of them mentioned her loss of memory but as the days passed, instead of easing, her need to know and understand him and their complex and puzzling relationship became more urgent.

On the last night of their honeymoon, her thoughts restless, she lay beside him in the big double bed. After a while, aware that he too was wakeful, she said quietly, 'Jos, won't you talk to me?'

'About what?'

'About us. If I only knew what you *wanted*...'

He answered sardonically, 'I thought I'd made that abundantly clear.'

She sighed. 'Yet I feel you resent me and despise yourself for wanting me...'

A barely perceptible stiffening told her she'd hit gold, but his voice was smooth as he mocked, 'Don't feminists assert that most men resent women?'

'So far as I know I'm not a feminist,' she said evenly.

When he stayed silent she pushed herself up on one elbow, and, peering down into his dark face in the half-light, said helplessly, 'I just don't understand you...'

His eyes gleamed between thick dark lashes as he stonewalled. 'How many people do understand their partners?'

She gritted her teeth. 'All I'm trying to do is make sense of our relationship. Without knowing or understanding, how can I have any faith in it?'

'Even relationships that are started with the best intentions sometimes become a test of blind faith.'

'But I don't even know what our intentions were...'

'Yours was to have a rich husband.'

Though she knew he was wrong, his words still had the power to hurt and agitate.

Taking a calming breath, she asked evenly, 'And *yours*?'

With a kind of bleak mockery that made her shiver, he said, 'I have very few scruples, and it's always been my intention to enslave you, to tie you to me with bonds of passion that would make it impossible for you to leave me.'

She found herself saying, 'Bonds of love would be stronger.' Again she sensed his lean body tense, and, knowing she was getting to him, she went on with growing confidence. 'Passion is relatively easy to come by, and therefore expendable.'

'But at least it exists.' He sounded angry.

'And you don't believe love does?'

'I have no reason to believe it.'

'Just because you missed out as a child, it doesn't mean...' She stopped and tried again. 'If you knew how love can—'

'But I don't. The only thing I know about love is how to live without it.'

She heard the desolation, the pain. Putting her palm against his cheek, she said softly, 'Jos, I've never told you what I feel for you—'

'Don't try and kid me you feel anything for me beyond desire and the gratification of knowing I can provide what you want.'

He rolled over suddenly, pinning her down with the weight of his body. 'The last thing I want from you is any pretence of love. Even if you hate me I'll make sure you enjoy my wealth and the kind of lifestyle you married me for.'

Filled with a kind of cold anguish, she asked bleakly, 'And what will you enjoy?'

But she already knew the answer to that. A sensual exploitation, a cynical ownership without respect or even liking…

He laughed harshly, and settled his lean hips into the cradle of hers. 'Surely you don't have to ask.'

Afterwards, lying listening to his even breathing, she found her mind rerunning the tape of their conversation, heard him saying again, '…it's always been my intention to enslave you, to tie you to me with bonds of passion that would make it impossible for you to leave me.'

But before he could start to weave those bonds she had left him…

Then she heard herself averring that bonds of love would be stronger.

But even with those bonds already in place she had still left him…

Why…? *Why?*

They set off for home the following day—Jos with his usual air of cool assurance, Clare with a feeling of anxiety that lay like a dark cloud over her spirits. Apart from any other consideration, what was she to *do* with herself all day in a penthouse flat that was already perfectly run?

As their plane headed for La Guardia she was aware of Jos's eyes fixed on her half averted face, before he leaned towards her and asked quietly, 'Something bothering you?'

Everything. 'Not really.'

'So tell me about it.' There was a look in his eyes that convinced her he meant to know.

She chose the simplest problem. 'I was just wondering how I was going to fill my time…I mean when you go back to work. I have no friends in New York, and you pay Roberts to take care of everything…'

He lifted a dark brow. 'You don't like the idea of being a lady of leisure?'

'No.'

'But you've never had what you might call a career,' he pointed out. 'In any case—'

'I'm useless until I get my memory back,' she broke in bitterly.

'That wasn't what I was going to say.'

'But it's the truth.'

'I hardly think so.' Though soft, his voice had an edge to it. 'In fact the last thing I'd call you is *useless*… And you show so much enthusiasm, such a willingness to learn.'

He watched the colour flood into her cheeks before going on, 'Of course, if you fancy yourself in the role of a shop assistant or a waitress, and you don't mind waiting in line for a job that someone else is going to need a great deal more than you do…'

The words hung sharp and hurtful in the air.

But though she accepted the justness of the latter half of his sentence, she fought back, low-voiced. 'Rather than have to sit alone in an empty apartment all day with nothing to do, I'd prefer it if I *was* a shop assistant or a waitress.'

'Well, I wouldn't,' he said shortly. 'And though you won't remember, when we first discussed it I made no secret of the fact that I didn't want a working wife, I wanted a full-time companion, someone who's there when I get home, who's free to travel with me at a moment's notice...'

'And what did *I* want?' Then she added bleakly, 'Apart from a rich husband, that is...'

'What *do* you want?'

A real home and a family, a husband who loves me, my memory back... She shook her head helplessly. 'If I just had a home to look after...'

'Do you want me to fire Roberts?'

'No, of course not. Even if you did—' She broke off abruptly.

'Even if I did...?'

Bracing herself, she spoke the truth. 'I couldn't think of the penthouse as home.'

Surprising her, he said, 'I've never thought of it as home either... But to return to the point you were making, you won't be sitting in the apartment alone all day with nothing to do. I've no intention of going straight back to work. In fact I plan to take an extended honeymoon while I show you around New York and introduce you to my friends.'

Had that been on the cards *before* her loss of memory? she wondered. Aloud, she asked, 'But are you able to take more time off?'

'One good point about being the boss is that you get to call the shots. I have an excellent staff. An occasional phone call or an hour at my desk should be enough to keep my affairs running smoothly...'

When she said nothing, he queried a shade sarcastically, 'Does that make you feel any better?'

Though well aware that what he'd outlined was a short-term solution—it didn't actually *solve* anything—perforce she nodded.

Seeming to know what she was thinking, he took her hand and went on, 'And I intend to make changes to our lifestyle in the not too distant future.'

'What kind of changes?' she asked uncertainly.

He lifted the hand he was holding and touched his lips to the delicate blue veins on the inside of her wrist. 'Sweeping ones.'

A passing stewardess, seeing the intimate little caress, sighed audibly, and gave Clare a quick, envious glance.

They arrived to find New York baking and airless, heat and humidity gripping the city like a sweaty fist. The smell of melting tar and hot metal mingled with dust and exhaust fumes. Perspiring pedestrians mopped their brows. Bus doors hissed open, sucked in limp passengers and hissed shut again. Even the bright yellow cabs had lost their briskness and assumed a lethargic air.

When they reached the penthouse, Roberts, balding and benign, was waiting to welcome them with glasses of fruit juice chinking with ice.

After expressing a polite hope that they'd had a good journey, he continued, 'Ms Dwyer has rung several times, sir.'

'What did she want?' Jos sounded far from pleased.

'Merely to enquire when you would be home,' Roberts said blandly. 'I told her you were expected back today, and she asked if you would call her as soon as you got in.'

Jos gave a curt nod.

Having announced that an evening meal would be ready shortly, the manservant deferred to Clare. 'Would madam prefer to eat in the dining room or on the terrace?'

It might be hot and muggy on the terrace, but she favoured the idea of eating in the open air rather than the air-conditioned sterility of the dining room.

'Oh, on the terrace, I think.' She glanced at Jos. 'If that's all right with you?'

'Of course,' he answered smoothly. Then he went on, 'If you'd like to go ahead and shower... I've a couple of business calls to make first.'

Did Ms Dwyer come under the heading of business? Clare wondered a shade waspishly as she made her way to the bedroom, then told herself not to be a fool. How could she feel jealous of some unknown woman who might even be married?

As though to emphasise the fact that they would now be sharing a room, Jos had carried both sets of luggage straight through to the bedroom and placed them side by side on a long chest.

The cross-eyed teddy bear he'd bought her, and which she'd refused to leave behind, was sitting a little drunkenly on her case.

Lifting him off, she imitated his expression before dropping a kiss on his black felt nose and putting him in the nearest chair.

As she did so Clare noticed that the light jacket Jos had taken off and slung casually over the chair-back had slipped to the floor.

It was the same one he'd worn the day they'd picnicked by the Niagara and crossed Rainbow Bridge into Canada.

All at once that seemed a long time ago.

Stooping, she picked up the jacket, and as she did so their passports slid out of one of the pockets and dropped onto the carpet. Jos's fell open, and a fleeting glimpse of something as the pages turned arrested her.

A frown marring her smooth forehead, Clare picked it up and took a closer look. The pictured face, with its handsome eyes and chiselled mouth, was familiar. But the accompanying name was strange.

Yet not strange.

Clave.

It seemed to jump out from the page at her. Staring down at it, she began to shake.

Clave…

A roaring sound filled her ears and she felt as though her head was bursting with the knowledge that somewhere, some time, way back in her childhood, perhaps, she had known a boy named Clave.

CHAPTER SIX

SHE was sure she hadn't liked him. She'd been afraid of him... But suddenly she was racked by a terrible feeling of guilt and regret.

Sinking into the chair, she covered her face with trembling hands and tried to think, but already the crack in the door was closing relentlessly, shutting out that tiny glimmer of light.

It took several minutes and a lot of will-power to pull herself together. When she felt calmer, she picked up her own passport and returned both of them to his pocket, before going into the bathroom on legs that still shook a little.

She was back in the bedroom, wearing a blue silk button-through dress but still barefoot, when Jos came in.

Careful not to look directly at him, she began to brush her hair, the dark, glossy cloud settling round a face that, despite its light tan, looked drained of colour and taut.

He'd taken off his shirt and footwear and was opening a drawer to find a change of clothing when, catching sight of her reflection in the mirror, he paused.

Turning, he put a hand beneath her chin and tilted her face up to his. Green eyes looked deep into violet and assessed the lingering agitation she was unable to hide. 'What's wrong?'

Some instinct warned her not to say anything until she'd had more time to think.

'Nothing.' She strove to look unconcerned.

His glance shadowed, yet intent, he ordered, 'Don't lie to me, Clare.'

'What makes you think I'm lying to you?'

When she would have turned away, he caught her arm and swung her back, holding her by the elbows. A little smile twisting his lips, he warned, 'If necessary I'm prepared to beat it out of you.'

It was a threat in spite of that smile, and she had a feeling he meant every word.

'Well?'

'Your jacket was lying on the floor. When I picked it up the passports slipped out of the pocket. Yours fell open...'

'And?' A dark brow lifted in interrogation.

Flustered, she said, 'Though I couldn't actually *remember*, I felt almost certain I'd once known someone with the same name...'

His face wiped clean of all expression, he remarked, 'Saunders is a fairly common name.'

'*Clave* isn't.'

His green eyes narrowed, leaving just a gleam of colour between the thick lashes, but he said nothing, merely watched her.

She went on haltingly, 'It seemed familiar... I associated it with my childhood...'

When he still said nothing, she asked, 'Why didn't you tell me your name was Clave?'

'Because I don't use that name.'

'Why not?'

He answered indirectly, 'I was christened Clave Joseph, after my grandfather. As you remarked, it isn't too common. After my parents died and I was sent to a state school, with a name like Clave and a ''posh'' accent you can imagine what kind of fun was poked at me.'

Almost wearily, he added, 'After I'd tried to fight half the school for chanting "Clavie" after me, I started to call myself Jos in self-defence. I've been Jos ever since.'

She felt a great sadness, a compassion that brought a lump to her throat.

His green eyes flared. Curtly, he said, 'I can do without your pity.'

Flushing, she told him briskly, 'That's good, because I wasn't going to give you any.'

He smiled with savage self-mockery. 'Don't tell me you weren't feeling sorry for me, thinking—'

'Shall I tell you what I *was* thinking?' Though thoroughly hot and bothered now, she lifted her chin and looked him in the eye, trying to meet the impact of his stare without flinching.

'Please do,' he invited, silkily sarcastic.

She took a deep breath while adrenalin pumped into her veins. 'I was thinking that at six foot three you're too big to carry a chip on your shoulder.'

The instant the words were spoken, she wished them unsaid.

For what seemed an age he stood quite still, his gaze heated and furious. Then, his anger masked, his tone as smoothly abrasive as pumice-stone, he said, 'I take great exception to that remark.'

'Because you think I'm wrong about the chip?'

'Because I think you're right.'

'Then you're not *too* angry?' She held her breath.

'Let's say that though I recognise the basic truth of your words, I still intend to make you pay for them.'

Before she could take evasive action, he swooped and threw her over his shoulder in a fireman's lift. 'There,

PLAY...

"ROLL A DOUBLE!"

PEEL OFF LABEL AND PLACE INSIDE

GET 2 BOOKS

AND A

FABULOUS MYSTERY BONUS GIFT

ABSOLUTELY *FREE!*

SEE INSIDE...

(U-H-P-11/98) 106 HDL CJRA

NO RISK, NO OBLIGATION TO BUY...NOW OR EVER!

GUARANTEED

PLAY "ROLL A DOUBLE" AND YOU GET FREE GIFTS! HERE'S HOW TO PLAY:

1. Peel off label from front cover. Place it in space provided at right. With a coin, carefully scratch off the silver dice. Then check the claim chart to see what we have for you – TWO FREE BOOKS and a mystery gift – ALL YOURS! ALL FREE!

2. Send back this card and you'll receive brand-new Harlequin Presents® novels. These books have a cover price of $3.75 each, but they are yours to keep absolutely free.

3. There's no catch. You're under no obligation to buy anything. We charge nothing – ZERO – for your first shipment. And you don't have to make any minimum number of purchases – not even one!

4. The fact is, thousands of readers enjoy receiving books by mail from the Harlequin Reader Service®. They like the convenience of home delivery...they like getting the best new novels BEFORE they're available in stores...and they love our discount prices!

5. We hope that after receiving your free books you'll want to remain a subscriber. But the choice is yours – to continue or cancel any time at all! So why not take us up on our invitation, with no risk of any kind. You'll be glad you did!

The Harlequin Reader Service®— Here's how it works:

Accepting free books places you under no obligation to buy anything. You may keep the books and gift and return the shipping statement marked "cancel." If you do not cancel, about a month later we'll send you 6 additional novels and bill you just $3.12 each, plus 25¢ delivery per book and applicable sales tax, if any.* That's the complete price — and compared to cover prices of $3.75 each — quite a bargain! You may cancel at any time, but if you choose to continue, every month we'll send you 6 more books, which you may either purchase at the discount price...or return to us and cancel your subscription.

*Terms and prices subject to change without notice. Sales tax applicable in N.Y.

If offer card is missing write to: Harlequin Reader Service, 3010 Walden Ave., P.O. Box 1867, Buffalo NY 14240-1867

BUSINESS REPLY MAIL
FIRST-CLASS MAIL   PERMIT NO. 717   BUFFALO, NY

POSTAGE WILL BE PAID BY ADDRESSEE

HARLEQUIN READER SERVICE
3010 WALDEN AVE
PO BOX 1867
BUFFALO NY 14240-9952

NO POSTAGE
NECESSARY
IF MAILED
IN THE
UNITED STATES

that should dislodge any chip. Now I think we both need to cool off.'

He was opening the bathroom door before she guessed his intention. 'No, Jos.' She began to struggle. 'I've already showered.'

Grimly jocular, he said, 'Not with me, you haven't.'

He turned the powerful jet full on, and, stepping beneath it, set her on her feet, hands gripping her shoulders, cold water pouring over them both.

Making no attempt to struggle now, she stood quietly, her hair a dark tangled mass of wet curls, her clothes plastered to her.

His eyes dropping to where her nipples were clearly visible through the thin material of her bodice, he enquired with mock solicitude, 'Not too cold?'

'Not at all,' she lied spiritedly, and, trying to stop her teeth chattering, added, 'I'm finding it quite refreshing.'

The effect was somewhat spoiled when a moment or two later she began to shiver.

He bent his head, and she felt his warm mouth close over a silk-clad nipple.

She continued to shiver, but for a different reason.

Reaching for the shower control, he turned it to comfortably hot, and with deft fingers began to unfasten the buttons that ran down the front of her dress. Then, slipping it from her shoulders, he tossed it aside before undoing her bra.

He claimed her mouth, deepening the kiss while he slid her clinging panties down over her hips and his fingers combed through the tangle of wet curls to find their goal and explore and stimulate with slow, rhythmic movements.

Steam began to swirl round them while those long, skilful fingers built a spiralling core of sensation.

Just as she felt herself arching helplessly towards him

he lifted his head and withdrew his hand, leaving her on the brink.

She bit her lip hard, determined not to show her feelings, not to let him manipulate her as though she was some puppet.

'Now it's your turn.' He took her hands and guided them to the waistband of his trousers.

Instead of immediately unfastening the clip, she ran her fingers over his chest, the golden skin smooth and slick except for the light sprinkling of wet black hair that arrowed in a V towards his stomach.

While the hot water continued to cascade over them she leaned forward and took one of the small flat nipples between her lips, stroking it with her tongue, tugging slightly, learning its resilience, its leathery texture, before closing her teeth on it with erotic delicacy.

He gave a kind of shudder.

Eyes closed, nuzzling her face across his chest, she searched for and found its twin while her fingers undid the clip and zipper and pushed the soaking trousers over lean hips.

As though the steamy heat had unfrozen the last of her inhibitions, with great deliberation she smoothed her palms down his flat stomach and her thumbs sketched slow arcs over the clinging silk shorts, before she sent them to follow the trousers.

When he'd stepped out of the garments and tossed them aside, her hand returned to caress the firm flesh she had freed.

When she heard his breath hiss sharply through his teeth, she smiled a small, triumphant smile. Now who was calling the tune?

Her satisfaction was short-lived.

Seizing her hand, he held it away from him, then, capturing the other, placed them both round his neck. A moment later he was lifting her, and, with his hands supporting her buttocks, urging, 'Wrap your legs around me, darling.'

When she did so, he smiled and guided her into position, his eyes glittering with a male triumph that even the pouring water and the wreathing steam couldn't conceal, before they went out of focus as he leaned forward to kiss her.

Afterwards they dried each other.

By the time they were both dressed they were late for the meal, and Clare tried not to dwell on what Roberts was bound to think when he found their saturated clothing.

Though out on the terrace it was warm, it was blessedly free from the dust and fumes encountered at street level. An electric fan whirred quietly, moving the still air, and the fountain, a delightful bronze of a pair of geese landing on the water with outstretched feet, was playing.

The splash and gurgle added to the impression of coolness, but, recalling the shower, Clare decided wryly that much more water and she'd develop webbed feet along with the geese.

Glancing up, she saw Jos's eyes were fixed on her, irony in their depths, as though he was reading her thoughts.

His face was too strong, too tough to be called conventionally handsome, but his mouth and his eyes, the arrangement of his features, his bone structure, made him compellingly attractive.

Even as an old man he would still be incredibly good to look at, she realised. But it was his eyes, brilliant, habitually mocking eyes, that never ceased to fascinate her.

Although she couldn't remember it, she could imagine

the impact when he had first looked at her with that cool, ironic gaze.

She must have been intrigued from the start, in fact he had remarked on it. But he'd described her response as 'cool reserve' so she must have also been instinctively scared, or at least *cautious* about getting involved with such a man.

Though now she could see clearly that she wouldn't have stood a chance when once he'd started to stalk her...

When once he'd started to stalk her...

Suddenly she shivered. The idea was so uncomfortable, so emotive, that she wondered what had made her subconsciously phrase the thought in such a way.

Something that had happened in the past? Something her subconscious knew that her conscious self couldn't remember? Something he was taking care not to tell her? Something to do with a boy named Clave?

After the shower, while Jos had dried her glowing body, he'd remarked teasingly, 'As a cooling off operation, this hasn't been a notable success...'

But as a diversionary tactic it had been highly successful.

Though if they *had* known each other as children why wouldn't he admit it? Unless there was something he wanted to keep hidden? Something that the name Clave Saunders might have recalled and that Jos Saunders didn't.

While she ate Clare struggled to get her thoughts in order, to find some answers, but all that emerged were more questions.

Had she known his name was Clave before she'd lost her memory? Had she recognised him as someone from her childhood? If she had, would she still have gone ahead and married him? Or had she only known him as Jos, and recollected nothing of any past involvement?

As he reached to refill her wine glass, she asked abruptly, 'Did I know your name was Clave before I lost my memory?'

The green eyes regarded her coolly. 'As I told you earlier, I haven't used the name since I was thirteen.'

She gritted her teeth and persisted, 'Then I only knew you as Jos?'

He answered obliquely, 'Our full names were used during the marriage service.'

Though if she had recognised it then, realised she had known him, she would have been already committed...

But that day at Niagara, when she had asked him if they had known each other as children, he had denied it. Or had he?

She thought back. After he'd remarked that he was surprised by how tender-hearted she'd grown up to be, she had asked, *Did* you know me?

There had been a short, but marked hesitation before he'd answered, 'I didn't need to know you. In my experience a lot of children can be heartless little monsters, and usually the females stay that way.'

So he hadn't actually denied it.

And now a growing conviction made her almost certain that they *had* known each other, that their paths had crossed in some disturbing way.

But *when* and *how*?

Summoning up all her courage and determination, more than tired of half-truths and evasions, Clare had opened her mouth to demand an unequivocal answer when, with a discreet cough, Roberts appeared.

'I'm sorry to disturb you, sir, but Ms Dwyer is on the phone asking to speak to you. I told her you had barely finished eating, but she was most insistent.'

Tossing down his napkin in a way that clearly indicated he wasn't too pleased at the interruption, Jos pushed back his chair and, saying curtly, 'You can serve the coffee,' preceded the manservant indoors.

The moment was irretrievably lost. Clare sighed. Now she would have to wait, screw up her courage all over again, before she could ask Jos what she wanted to know.

And even then there was no guarantee that he'd tell her. If, for whatever reason, he didn't want her to know the truth, he was quite capable of lying...

A minute or so later Roberts returned, grave and deferential, carrying a round silver tray with a pot of coffee and a dish of Turkish delight.

'This confection is Mr Saunders favourite, but if madam would prefer mints...?'

'No, I love Turkish delight.' *I love Turkish delight...I love Turkish delight...* As though spoken into an empty biscuit tin the words echoed hollowly inside her head, while, as if she was looking through the unfocused lens of a camera, her brain produced a blurred picture of a boy with dark hair and a thin face holding out a brightly coloured octagonal box.

Gripped by a kind of sick excitement, she strove to hold onto the picture, to bring it into focus, but abruptly it was gone.

She stifled a groan, but something of her mental turmoil must have been evident, because Roberts was asking with concern, 'Is anything wrong, madam?'

'No, I'm fine, thank you.' She managed a smile. 'Just a slight headache.'

Having filled her small cup, he placed the pot and the silver dish within reach and departed noiselessly.

Hoping that it would retrigger the memory, Clare helped herself to a piece of the delectable sweetmeat and chewed slowly, but while her saliva glands sprang into operation her brain stubbornly refused to co-operate.

Disappointed, she was licking the fine sugar from her fingers when Jos came back. His handsome face expressionless, he told her, 'We've been invited to a party.'

'Oh…'

He picked up the coffee-pot and filled his cup. 'I've accepted for us both. I hope you don't mind?'

Though well aware that the 'I hope you don't mind' had been added out of politeness, she nevertheless answered, 'No…' Then, appreciating that she'd sounded a little doubtful, she said more positively, 'No, of course I don't mind. When?'

'As soon as we've finished our coffee.'

Feeling a sudden flutter of panic, she objected, 'But I can't go to a party looking like this.'

His gaze lingered on the heart-shaped face that was free of make-up, on the cloud of dark curly hair and the winged brows, the violet eyes and flawless skin, the short, straight nose, high, slanting cheekbones and the disproportionately wide mouth, before travelling assessingly over the slender figure in a grey chiffon dress with a simple cross-over bodice and a full skirt.

A flame leapt in his green eyes. 'Every man there will envy me.'

Feeling a little flush of heat, she persisted even so, 'But I'm not dressed for a party.'

'What you have on looks fine to me. It's a fairly laid-back affair. I'm going as I am.'

Wearing well-cut casual trousers and a dark green silk shirt open at the neck, his cool elegance was enhanced by the kind of magnetism that was only partly sexual. It was his basic self-confidence, Clare decided, his aura of strength and authority that rounded off his powerful attraction.

'I thought it was about time I introduced my wife to some of my friends and acquaintances, and this is a perfect opportunity.'

Reaching for the coffee-pot once more, he raised an enquiring brow.

Playing for time, she nodded. 'Please.'

When he'd poured them both another cup, he went on, 'Tom Dwyer is a merchant banker; he lives in this same building a few floors down. He's both a friend and a business associate, so we know many of the same people.'

'And Ms Dwyer is his wife?'

'Tom's a widower. Andrea is his daughter.'

'And your mistress?' The words popped out without her conscious volition.

'Ex-mistress,' Jos corrected coolly.

Remembering the phone calls, Clare asked sweetly, 'Does *she* know that?'

'Jealous?'

Yes! 'No. I was just wondering if you'd got round to telling her.'

His face cold, almost disdainful, he said, 'I played by the rules. I told her it was finished before I went over to England.'

Repelled by what she saw as his heartlessness, Clare felt sorry for the other woman.

'There's no need to look so outraged.'

Aware that they shared no common ground, that he was a sophisticated man who held cynical views on relationships between the sexes, she said stiffly, 'That's a matter of opinion.'

A muscle tightened in his jaw. 'It was agreed from the start that there should be no commitments, and that either one of us could end the association without recriminations.'

Except that Andrea hadn't wanted to. Clare knew that as surely as if he'd admitted it aloud.

'To reinforce the fact that it *was* ended, and so there should be not the slightest doubt about my intentions, I told her as soon as we got engaged.'

'Over the phone?'

'Do you think I should have travelled all the way back to New York to break the news?'

'No, but... Well, it seems so *unfeeling*.'

He laughed derisively. 'Don't get it into your head that *feelings* were involved. She's a pretty cool lady, and it was a convenient arrangement that suited us both. Nothing more or less.'

Watching Clare's expressive face, he said, 'Look, let me put things into perspective for you. Andrea's only about your age and she's already had two husbands and a string of lovers. As far as I know she hasn't cared a jot for any of them, so I shouldn't waste too much sympathy on her.'

'I wasn't... But I don't like the idea of going to a party in her apartment.'

'Andrea has her own place when she cares to use it. This is her father's apartment.'

'I still find it hard to believe that she'd want me there,' Clare objected doggedly.

'*I* want you there.' His handsome face was hard, uncompromising, and his eyes held a steely glitter. 'When Andrea first mentioned a party, I told her that if I came I'd be bringing my wife.'

Her voice accusing, Clare said, 'You just want to use me to get her off your back.'

'Would you rather I allotted you alternate nights?'

'You're a brute!' she muttered hoarsely.

Appearing unmoved, he said, 'I may be a brute, but you're quite wrong about me wanting to use you. I'm more than capable of discouraging any woman who looks like becoming a nuisance. The problem I have with Andrea is that her father is a good friend of mine, and I don't want him to be hurt.'

'Then perhaps you shouldn't have chased after her in the first place.'

'At the risk of sounding ungallant, I must tell you that it was Andrea who did all the chasing...'

'Oh...' Clare said a little blankly.

'In case you hadn't realised,' he added sardonically, 'females are often more predatory than males. Your own mother was a prime example.'

She flushed painfully.

Watching her face grow hot, he swallowed the last of his coffee and rose to his feet. 'Ready?'

She shook her head. 'I won't go.'

'You will.'

His determination beat against her like an iron fist.

'I have no intention of going without you, so we can do this the easy way or the hard way... Whichever, the end result will be the same.'

'Please, Jos...'

Ignoring her plea, his face implacable, he held out his hand. 'Now, are you going on your own two feet or do I have to throw you over my shoulder?'

'I abhor caveman tactics,' she muttered mutinously. But, knowing he was quite capable of carrying out his threat, and unwilling to be humiliated, she rose and let him take her hand.

Tucking it through his arm, he glanced down at her set face and offered, 'We needn't stay long if you don't want to.' She was just breathing a sigh of relief, when he added ironically, 'They'll no doubt put our eagerness for an early night down to the fact that we're newly married.'

They were stepping out of the lift outside the Dwyers' apartment when Clare voiced the question that had been bothering her. 'Do they…do any of them know I've lost my memory?'

His finger on the door-bell, Jos said, 'Tom does. No one else, unless he's told them.'

The door was opened by a casually dressed, pleasant-looking man with a thick thatch of grey-blond hair. He seemed startled when he saw Clare, and she wondered with a sinking heart if she hadn't really been expected.

Switching his gaze to Jos, he exclaimed, 'Hi! Glad you folks could make it at such short notice. Come on in.'

Inside the opulent apartment there was a crowd of people and the talk and laughter of a party in full swing.

Clapping Jos on the shoulder, he went on, 'I understand Andrea's been trying to get hold of you…'

Clare noticed the faintest shadow of unease flit across his face as he mentioned Andrea.

'We've been away on honeymoon,' Jos told him easily. 'Just got back a couple of hours ago.'

His arm around Clare's waist, he made the introductions. 'Darling, this is our host… Tom, my wife, Clare…'

Tom Dwyer was a lean, rangy man in his early fifties, Clare judged, with level blue eyes and a firm handshake. 'It's nice to meet you,' he said, sounding as if he wanted to mean it. Then, glancing up, 'Ah, here's Andrea.'

'Darling!' A tall, slender woman with shining blonde hair and a dress like blue lightning appeared from the throng and made as if to throw her arms around Jos's neck and kiss him full on the lips.

He was took quick for her. Catching her wrists, he held her away, and when, after a second or two, mortified colour began to creep into her face, bent his dark head to give her a chaste peck on the cheek.

'How are you, Andrea? You're looking very well...'

That was a blatant understatement.

Andrea was dazzling and glamorous, blessed with a marvellous figure, and only a certain hardness detracted from what was still a stunning beauty.

'This is my wife, Clare...'

The blonde carried off the snub admirably. 'Having a new wife has made you very formal,' she rebuked Jos gaily, and for the first time took her attention from him and transferred it to Clare.

As she did so the pale blue eyes widened and gazed almost in disbelief, before the bright lips twisted into a smile as false as her greeting. 'I'm so pleased you could come. Do forgive me for staring, but you remind me of someone...'

A waiter appeared with a loaded tray.

'Champagne?' Tom Dwyer put a glass in Clare's hand and one in Joe's, before serving his daughter and himself.

'What are we celebrating?' Jos enquired idly as they stood sipping the sparkling wine.

Andrea answered. 'My divorce, darling. The decree absolute has just come through.'

She gave Clare another smile which, though brilliant, left her eyes as cold as chips of blue ice. 'I hope you don't mind me calling your husband darling, but you see, we're old friends.'

'Yes, I know,' Clare said quietly.

'Oh, really?' Though not excessively loud, Andrea's voice was pitched to carry. 'I thought your mind had gone funny, that you couldn't remember anything...'

Several people glanced furtively in their direction.

Feeling like some freak, but determined not to show

she was upset, Clare had just schooled her face into careful blandness when Tom said hurriedly, 'Jos told me you hit your head when you were knocked down by a cab?'

'That's right.' She smiled at him, trying to ease his obvious embarrassment. 'I can't remember anything that happened *before* the accident, but hopefully the amnesia will pass.'

'There's nothing you can do?'

'Nothing but wait.' Her voice was level. 'No effort of will seems able to bring my memory back, so I've just got to make the best of things.'

'Suppose it never comes back?' Andrea gave a mock shudder. 'Poor you. I've always had a dread of being *abnormal*... I really don't know how you'll cope...'

Sensing that the blonde was trying to get at Jos through her rather than making a personal attack, Clare said mildly, 'Oh, I think I'll manage to struggle along. I just won't have any recollection of my childhood or growing up.'

'How awful. And no memories of your wedding day—'

'There's a lot of people who would be only too pleased to forget *that*,' Tom broke in, clearly uncomfortable.

Turning to Jos, Andrea persisted, 'You must find it terribly upsetting, having a wife who's not quite... I mean, who's lost her memory.'

Smiling down at Clare, Jos dropped a light kiss on the corner of her mouth and drawled, 'Not at all. You see, it makes her mine in a very special way.'

Andrea's tinkling laugh sounded forced. 'I don't quite follow...'

'There are no memories of any other men to come between us.'

The pale blue eyes bright with malice, Andrea said

smoothly, 'I expect Clare wishes that would work in reverse.'

Just as smoothly, Jos murmured, 'I have to say that none of the women in my past have been memorable enough to intrude.'

Little coins of colour appeared on Andrea's beautifully made-up face.

Wishing the floor would open and swallow her up, Clare tried to think of something innocuous to say—and failed miserably.

Though inwardly admitting that Andrea should have had more sense than to goad him, she felt sorry for the other woman, and regretted Jos's deliberate cruelty.

The doorbell enabled Tom to rescue the situation. Turning to his daughter, he said hastily, 'While I see who that is, can you go and be nice to the congressman's wife? She doesn't know many people here and she's looking a bit out of things.'

'Certainly.' A smile pinned to her lips, and ignoring Jos completely, Andrea suggested to Clare, 'When you've had a chance to mix a bit, perhaps we could get together for a chat?'

Wondering why the blonde wanted to talk to her, and her heart sinking at the prospect, Clare nevertheless said, 'Of course,' and managed to return the smile.

When the other two had gone, Jos slanted her a glance. 'Do you really want a tête-à-tête with Andrea?'

'No. But as she seems to be our hostess, what else could I say?'

'Those good manners will be the death of you.' He sounded half-amused, half-irritated. 'And she's such a bitch, I don't know why you feel the need to be kind.'

'It's better than being cruel.'

'Andrea won't appreciate it. In her book, kindness equates with weakness.'

'But not in mine,' Clare said firmly.

Jos sighed, and, having disposed of their glasses on an occasional table, said, 'As soon as we've said hello to a few people, we can leave.'

'And let her think I'm running away?'

He half shook his head. 'She's out to hurt you.'

'Why should *you* care, when—?' Clare broke off.

'When I'm not always kind to you myself?' He hesitated, then said slowly, 'Perhaps I prefer to be the one to hurt you, to make you bleed.' Watching a shiver run through her, he added flatly, 'If you stay and fight, she'll rout you.'

'Do you think so?'

He looked down at her, at the steady violet eyes, the firm mouth and stubborn chin. 'No, I don't. I'm underrating you. Despite your gentleness, your soft-heartedness, you have plenty of courage and strength.

'Come no, then.' He tucked her hand through his arm and, looking cool, slightly formidable, said, 'Let's go and circulate.'

At the end of perhaps an hour, Clare had met nearly all the people there. Though she had made an effort, she was ashamed to admit that she'd already forgotten most of their names.

Many of them had looked surprised when Jos had introduced her as his wife, and several of the females had said how unexpected it all was, and tried to hide their regret that he was no longer an eligible bachelor.

He had just presented Clare to a small group of financiers from Wall Street, when Scott Wendell, a young man with a weak chin and the beginnings of a paunch, burst out, 'Do you know, I thought for a minute—'

Catching Jos's eye, he stopped abruptly, before continuing a shade awkwardly, 'Well, I must say you kept that very quiet, you sly fox.' Then he turned to Clare.

'And he tried to tell us that his visit to England was a business trip.'

She smiled, 'Well, I gather it was.'

Clearly a ladies' man, Wendell said gallantly, 'Speaking as someone who makes similar trips, I wish *I* could do that well for myself during the course of business... Oh, and with regard to business,' he went on, just as Andrea joined the little group, 'had you heard that Clemensons's Bank is—?'

'If you men are going to talk business,' the blonde broke in, 'we'll leave you to it.' Slipping a hand through Clare's arm, she added with a smile that was about as friendly as a clenched fist, 'There's something I'd like to show you...'

As they moved away Wendell could be heard to say succinctly, 'Her claws, no doubt.'

CHAPTER SEVEN

APART from a tightening of the carmine lips, Andrea gave no sign that she'd heard as she led Clare away from the noise and laughter of the party and into a small library-cum-study.

A tray of drinks stood at one side. After splashing bourbon into a couple of glasses, she added ice and handed one to Clare, waving her to a brocade-covered couch.

Dropping into the chair opposite, the blonde took a long swallow of her drink and said without preamble, 'I suppose you know that I was going to marry Jos when he came back to the States?'

'No, I didn't,' Clare said quietly.

'I was only waiting for my divorce to go through.'

'Did *he* know that?'

Almost defiantly, Andrea said, 'At that time there was no other woman in his life and I understood his needs.'

'I take it you're referring to his sexual needs?'

'Don't kid yourself he has any others.'

'Doesn't everyone?'

'He's as tough and impervious as they come, with no room for softer feelings or emotional commitments. I don't pretend that he loved me—I doubt if he's loved any woman—and he can be a cruel swine, but he's the only man I've ever gone overboard for, and we could have made a go of it if it hadn't been for you.'

Feeling an unwilling sympathy for the woman, Clare

said, 'He told me the affair was over before he left for England.'

Her nails crimson talons against the glass, the blonde tossed back her drink and reached to pour herself another. 'I could have changed his mind if you hadn't set out to hook him.'

'But I didn't set out to hook him.'

'I thought you couldn't remember.'

'Jos told me. He said I hadn't used my wiles to catch him.'

'And he's some catch. Even if he wasn't filthy rich he'd still be every woman's dream. I take it you didn't marry him for his money?'

'He thinks I did.'

Andrea raised a beautifully plucked brow. 'So when you stuck out for a wedding ring he was ready to buy you... How did you manage it so he thought you hadn't used your wiles? Did you hold back? Play hard to get? Make him believe you were an untouched English rose? Jos is the kind of man who would enjoy a challenge, and perhaps the idea of breaking new ground held a special appeal for him. Did he think you were a virgin and—?'

'Hardly,' Clare said drily.

'Then why do you suppose he married you?'

'He wanted me.'

'Well, that makes us equal. So when the bloom has worn off we might end up sharing him for a while, before you get your final marching orders.'

'I doubt it.'

Her lip curling, Andrea said almost pityingly, 'You don't believe he'll tire of you?'

Clare shook her head. 'I mean I wouldn't share him.' With sudden passionate intensity, she added, 'I *couldn't*.'

The blonde's eyes narrowed. 'Anyone would think you loved him.'

'I do.'

'Then I'm sorry for you. He won't want your love. He's a hard-as-nails, self-sufficient bastard, and if you imagine for one minute that he cares about you…'

All at once weary, sick to death of this futile tête-à-tête, Clare said, 'I don't imagine he cares about me.' She put her untouched drink on the table, slopping it a little, clumsy in her agitation. 'Now, if you'll excuse me, I think I'll go back to the party.'

'But we haven't finished our conversation, and I still have something to show you.' Andrea's voice was light, almost friendly, but her face looked cold and tight.

Shaking her head, Clare rose to her feet. 'All this is pointless…'

'Far from it.' The pale blue eyes glittered with triumph. 'Shall I tell you the *real* reason Jos married you?'

Suddenly aware that this was the whole purpose of the get-together, what the other woman had been leading up to, Clare asked with studied calmness, 'Are you sure you know it?'

'Oh, I know it all right. Though I didn't fully realise until I *saw* you and discovered just how like her you are. Of course, you haven't got her kind of glamour, her stunning sexual aura—in fact it's like comparing a watercolour to an oil painting—but still the likeness is strong, wouldn't you say?'

'I haven't the faintest idea what you're talking about…'

As though Clare hadn't spoken, Andrea went on, 'While she was visiting New York he became infatuated with her, and I think it must have come as a real shock when she died…'

'Died?' Clare echoed, dry-mouthed. Beginning to

understand. Not wanting to understand. 'How did she die? When did she die?'

'A few months ago in a plane crash in Panama.'

Clare's palms grew clammy and her stomach tied itself into a knot of tension as Andrea went on.

'I knew Jos needed a woman, and that was when I went to him. With the opposition out of the way, I thought he'd be mine.' Bitterly, she added, 'But his obsession obviously hadn't been cured, and he must have decided that if he wasn't able to have the mother, he'd have the daughter...'

Her knees turning to jelly, Clare sank back onto the couch. Scarcely above a whisper, she said, 'I don't believe you. He didn't even know my mother—at least not personally.'

'He knew her, believe me. When he first saw her picture in the papers he couldn't hide his interest, and, though she must have been a good twelve years older than he was, as soon as they met he became her lover. He was so fascinated by her that for weeks he scarcely let her out of his sight...'

The blood pounded in Clare's ears and sweat broke out on her forehead. So she had been just a substitute. Was that why Jos sometimes appeared to hate and resent her? Because she was alive while her mother was dead?

No, surely not. If he seemed at times to hate *her*, he'd almost certainly hated her mother more. It had been implicit in his look and his voice every time he'd mentioned her.

'I don't believe you,' Clare repeated more firmly, certain now that the blonde was just out to make trouble. 'He didn't even like her.'

'Perhaps that's what he wanted you to believe. But does this look as though he didn't like her?' Taking a glossy magazine from one of the drawers in the bureau,

Andrea tossed it onto the couch. 'Have a look at the society gossip pages.'

Trying to keep her hand steady, Clare opened *Jet Set* and flicked through it until she found what she was looking for.

Staring up at her from the shiny double-page spread was a full-length picture of a slender dark-haired woman with a Sophia Loren type of face.

A face that was familiar to her…

But was her sudden shock of recognition due to the fact that the face, apart from its hollow-cheeked gauntness and the age difference, which was evident even through the make-up, could have been her own?

Wearing an ankle-length black sheath, slashed almost to the thigh, the woman was clinging to Jos's arm while he, devastatingly handsome in impeccable evening dress, was looking down at her.

Clare read the caption.

Wealthy banker Jos Saunders is seen here escorting Lady Isobel Berkeley, the wife of diplomat Sir Roger Berkeley, to Culpeppers. Later in the evening they were spotted dancing cheek to cheek at the Pelican Club…and, in the early hours of the morning, engaged in cementing Anglo-American relations…

The accompanying photographs showed the pair first entwined on the dance floor and then sitting at a table, their dark heads close together, their mouths clinging.

Feeling as though she was slowly bleeding to death, Clare read on.

It has been rumoured that Lady Berkeley, previously known for her somewhat wild lifestyle, has ditched all her former admirers in favour of the handsome banker…

She stared at the caption, re-reading it until the print danced before her eyes, before returning her gaze to the damning photographs and marvelling at how alike her mother and she had been…

No wonder Andrea had done a double-take on meeting her for the first time, and so many other people had looked surprised!

It was a miracle no one had said anything… But of course, Scott Wendell had started to blurt it out, and had been stopped by Jos's cool, repressive glance…

So now she knew why Jos had married her, and Andrea was right. Still obsessed by a woman he could no longer have, he'd settled for her daughter because of a strong physical resemblance.

Could that have been what she'd discovered after their wedding? Was that why she had left him?

Closing the magazine, feeling oddly numb, detached, as though she was herself a bloodless corpse, she got to her feet and, vaguely surprised that her legs would support her, heard herself saying stiffly, 'If you don't mind, I'll go now.'

At the same instant there was a rap on the door and it opened.

Jos glanced from one woman to the other, then his narrowed green gaze returned to rest on Clare's taut white face. 'Ready to leave, darling?'

'Yes, I'm ready.' In her own ears her voice sounded thin and strained.

She allowed him to put his arm around her waist and lead her out and through the throng, walking by his side like a zombie.

One or two people said goodnight as they passed, and she answered automatically.

Tom, his blue eyes showing a marked anxiety, popped up from nowhere to escort them to the door. 'Pity you have to go so soon. Hope to see you before too long.'

'Yes, of course,' she answered meaninglessly, and, taking his proffered hand, even managed a smile.

Not until they reached the penthouse did Jos say almost curtly, 'I'm sorry you found the tête-à-tête with Andrea distressing, but I did warn you what to expect.'

Clare looked up at him, her gaze curiously dark and blind, and all at once the false calm deserted her and she began to tremble uncontrollably.

With a muttered oath, Jos picked her up in his arms and carried her through to their bedroom. He laid her down on the bed. Her eyes were tightly closed, her whole body shaking.

Having slipped off her sandals, he started to undress her. Despite the heat, her skin felt cold, and he pulled the lightweight duvet over her before stripping off his own clothes and getting in beside her.

She had stopped shaking now, and was lying quiet and still as a corpse, her face turned away from him.

When he attempted to draw her close and warm her cold flesh with his own, she suddenly came to life and began to fight like a tigress, crying fiercely, 'Get out and leave me alone... Leave me alone... I won't sleep in the same bed with you.'

Without loosening his hold on her upper arms, he demanded roughly, 'What is it? What did that bitch say to you?'

'Take your hands off me.' Beside herself, she struck at him repeatedly, savagely. 'I don't want you to touch me. I hate you! I hate you!'

Her clenched fist caught him a glancing blow high on his cheekbone and he released his grip, but only to catch hold of her wrists and pin them to the pillow.

'Let me go!' she spat at him.

'Not until you're through acting like a wild cat.'

When she continued to struggle and thrash about he held her, using one muscular leg to trap hers, so that she could hurt neither of them until, totally exhausted, her breath coming in harsh gasps, she lay still.

He looked down at her in the half-light, his own breath coming quickly, a lock of dark hair falling over his forehead. 'Now, suppose you tell me what all that was about?'

'Please let go of me.' Her voice was hoarse, rasping; her throat felt sore.

His expression wary, as though he was half expecting another onslaught, he let her go and sat up.

Moving as far away from him as the bed would allow, she pushed herself up against the pillows and turned to look at him, her eyes brilliant with anger.

'Well?' He raised a dark brow.

'You lied to me. If not directly, then by omission. When I asked if you knew my mother, you said you knew *of* her. You pretended to hate her.'

'That was no pretence. I *did* hate her.'

'You can save yourself the trouble of lying any more. I know that while she was in New York you became infatuated with her.'

'You're quite wrong.'

'You were her lover.'

His voice like ice, he said, 'I was *never* her lover.'

Furiously, she cried, 'It's no use trying to deny it. I *know*.'

He gave an elaborate sigh. 'I hope you didn't believe everything Andrea told you?'

'I believe the evidence of my own eyes. I read the society gossip and saw the pictures of you and my mother in *Jet Set*.'

She saw him stiffen. 'So that rubbish was what Andrea wanted to show you.'

'But it isn't rubbish, is it? And now I know why you married me.'

He looked at her, his eyes narrowed to green slits. 'Then perhaps you'd like to tell me?'

'Because my mother was dead and I look like her. That was why I left you, wasn't it? I found out that I was just a substitute...'

'That wasn't the reason at all.'

Ignoring his denial, she rushed on, 'Well, I won't be *used*. I won't be a stand-in for any woman, let alone my own mother. I'm leaving you.'

There was a moment of ominous silence before he said mildly, 'Don't be foolish, Clare.'

'I mean it.'

'Where would you go?'

'I don't know... Anywhere would be better than staying here.'

'You have no money. No means of supporting yourself.'

'I'll get a job—manage somehow.'

He shook his head. 'I've no intention of letting you leave. And you know you don't really want to.'

His arrogant confidence infuriated her. 'I do want to. I'm going first thing in the morning.'

'I think not.'

'You can't stop me.'

'Oh, yes I can.' His absolute certainty made her blood run cold.

Trying not to shiver, she asked defiantly, 'Wouldn't Roberts think it strange if you kept me locked in?'

'If necessary I'll have you restrained in a private clinic. All I need to do is contact Dr Hauser and tell him that as well as leaving you with amnesia, the blow to your head has made you…shall we say…unstable. That you refuse to stay with me and you're not able to take care of yourself.'

She looked at him in horror. 'You *wouldn't*…'

'I'd rather not. But unless you're willing to see sense…'

'You're a swine,' she said jerkily.

'I'm your husband.'

She stiffened. 'Well, you might be able to make me stay—' at least for the time being, she qualified silently '—but I've no intention of sleeping with you.'

His smile was mocking, reminiscent. 'I don't think I'll have too much trouble changing you mind. Last time—'

'That was before I knew I was merely an understudy for my mother.'

'Jealous?'

'No, I'm not jealous!' Her voice shook. 'But it's…it's disgusting and degrading.'

'It might be if it were true. But you're nothing of the kind.'

Ignoring the denial, she demanded, her voice rising, 'Do you think of *her*, see *her* face while you're making love to me?'

'I haven't so far.' His voice had an edge that should have warned her. 'But we'll try again, shall we?'

'No! I don't want you.'

'You know perfectly well that's a lie. You *do* want me.'

She felt an urge to fly at him, to rake her nails down that hard, arrogant face. 'Well, if you think I'm going to fight my mother's ghost for a place in your bed…'

'We're in my bed now, and I'll be happy to prove that if your mother's ghost does share it, it's not in the role of ex-mistress…'

Hands gripping her waist, he pulled her further down the bed and held her with steely fingers.

'And just to give you confidence that her features aren't superimposed on yours, I won't even look at your face and I'll keep saying your name.'

With a sudden movement she was unprepared for, he rolled her onto her stomach and used the weight of his body to pin her there.

Disregarding her muffled protest, he brushed aside the cloud of dark silky hair and put his lips to her nape, his breath warm against her skin.

Clare lay rigid, such intimate contact with the full length of his body making the blood rush through her veins. She could feel his heart thudding into her back, his crisp body hair against the smoothness of her skin, the roughness of his legs along hers, and the ripple of each muscle whenever he moved.

Her response was immediate and electric.

At first his mouth roving over the back of her neck remained gentle, his tongue exploring the hollow behind her ear with sensuous appreciation, but soon the kisses were interspersed with little bites and nibbles.

As she gasped, and tried to evade such erotic torment, he slid his hands beneath her to cup her breasts and tease the nipples while he moved rhythmically, mimicking the thrust of possession.

Fire flashed through her and a core of molten heat began to form low in her abdomen. She gave a little moan.

'Let me know when you're ready for the real thing,' he whispered.

'No,' she gasped hoarsely. 'I don't...I won't...'

'Ah, but you *do*, and you *will*, my darling wife.'

He was ruthless in his mastery, and even when she was almost sobbing, a victim of the dark sensuality he'd unleashed, he made her beg for release from the exquisite torture he was so good at inflicting.

Then, sliding his hands down to lift her body a little, and repeating her name as he'd promised, he made love to her with maddening slowness until she was finally engulfed by such a torment of delight that her whole body felt boneless, just a shuddering mass of sensations.

When he moved away from her she lay quite still, her face buried in the pillow. Hating him for his arrogant domination. Hating herself for her own humiliating lack of will-power where he was concerned.

'Turn over and look at me.'

She wanted to ignore the order, but somehow she found herself obeying. Turning over stiffly, reluctantly, she sat up, and, drawing her knees close to her chest, hugged them defensively beneath the duvet while her violet eyes met and clashed with Jos's green.

Studying her through half-closed lids, he said, 'I hope I've established that you *do* want me, and that I don't think of any other woman while I'm making love to you?'

'As far as I'm concerned, the only thing you have established—apart from the fact that you're utterly ruthless—is that in some form or other my mother's ghost *does* share the bed. Even if it isn't as your ex-mistress... Though after seeing that magazine I find it almost impossible to believe you weren't lovers.'

'It happens to be the truth.'

'How can I credit anything you tell me?' she cried helplessly. 'You lead me to believe you didn't know her, then I see a picture of you kissing her passionately...'

'Not to put too fine a point on it, *she* was kissing *me*.'

'I don't see what difference it makes,' Clare said wearily.

'A great deal of difference.'

'That's just sophism. You said you hated her, but those photographs and what Andrea told me prove otherwise.'

'What exactly did she tell you?'

'That when you first saw my mother's picture in the paper you couldn't hide your interest, and that despite the age difference as soon as the pair of you met you became lovers—'

'As I don't go in for three in a bed, how could Andrea know a thing like that? At best it's mere supposition.'

Ignoring the interruption, Clare ploughed on, 'She said you were so fascinated by her that you scarcely let her out of your sight. And even though that gossip column goes to prove it, I suppose you're going to try and tell me that it's not the truth.'

'Part of it is,' he admitted flatly. 'I was more than interested when I first saw your mother's picture in the paper. It aroused the kind of feelings that might have been best left buried. Telling myself she'd go to the devil anyway, I tried to put her out of my mind, but without much success.' He sounded grim. 'In fact she became almost an obsession.

'I made certain that our paths crossed. I wanted to take a closer look at the woman I'd loathed for years, to find out for sure if she really was the kind of tramp I'd always thought her.'

He paused for so long that Clare was forced to ask, 'And was she?'

'Oh, yes.' His teeth gleamed in a smile that was more like a snarl. 'If I hadn't hated her so much, I could almost have felt sorry for her, for what she'd become.'

'But you must have had some *reason* to feel so strongly about her. I can't believe it was just because you disapproved of her lifestyle.'

'Oh, I certainly had a reason.'

'Then don't you think it's time you told me what it was? Told me what she'd done to make you hate her so much?'

Clare held her breath until he said abruptly, 'Yes, perhaps you should know exactly what kind of bitch your mother was... We'd scarcely been introduced when, despite the fact that her husband was looking on, she made a dead set at me. It was so blatant it was sickening.

'She wanted me to take her to bed that first night, but I refused on the grounds that I didn't fancy being one of a string of lovers, and I had grave reservations about accepting what she offered while her husband was on the scene.

'She said, "If the thought of me having other lovers bothers you, I'll give them up, and as for my *husband*, so long as there's no *open* scandal, believe me, he wouldn't care a damn."'

'Oddly enough, I *did* believe her. I suppose, over the years, he must have become inured to her goings-on. But I told her that in the circumstance I wasn't prepared to cuckold him. Though, God forgive me, I was tempted. She had the kind of beauty that can drive a man out of his mind. I knew only too well how immoral and unscrupulous she was, but I still had to fight the pull of her physical attraction when she tried to seduce me.'

Through stiff lips, Clare asked, 'Then why did you keep on seeing her?'

His face hardened into a ruthless mask. 'Because knowing I'd been right about her all along had revived all my old desire for revenge. But I needed time to decide on the best way to make her pay, in some small way, for what she'd done. And by then, possibly because I'd refrained from taking her to bed, she seemed to be besotted with me...'

Oh, yes, Clare thought, and knew a kind of bleak empathy. She could imagine the hunger that must have clawed at a woman of her mother's temperament.

'She said she had to accompany her husband on a diplomatic mission to Panama, but that after they returned, while Sir Roger went to Washington, she would come and join me in New York... I made up my mind that when she did, after I'd told her exactly what I thought of her, I would drop her as publicly as possible. But, as you know, fate stepped in...'

And if it hadn't he would no doubt have carried out his plan to publicly humiliate a woman he admitted he'd hated.

A woman she couldn't remember; a woman of whom she'd heard nothing but ill; a woman for whom, she was shaken to realise, she suddenly felt a strong compassion, even a wish to defend.

Trying to hide her agitation, Clare said, 'You still haven't told me why you hated her so much.'

If only he would tell her that, she would have the key to his behaviour, would know what all these dark undercurrents meant.

Jos's eyes were thoughtful as they watched her hand, slender and restless, repeatedly smoothing the duvet over her knees.

He answered with a question of his own. 'Seeing a picture of your mother didn't bring anything back?'

'No.'

'You've had no flashes of memory?'

'When I first saw the name Clave in your passport it was familiar, and I felt as if I was on the brink of recalling something important. But all I could think was that somewhere, some time—in my childhood, perhaps—I'd know a boy named Clave.'

'That's *all* you remembered?' Jos's question was sharp.

'I… I was sure I hadn't liked him. I'd been afraid of him… Then suddenly I had an awful feeling of guilt and regret…'

Just for an instant Jos's dark face seemed to be full of pain and anguish, but the look vanished so swiftly that she wondered if she'd only imagined it.

'Nothing else?' he asked, more gently.

'When Roberts brought in some Turkish delight with the coffee he asked if I would prefer mints, and I said, No, I love Turkish delight. The words seemed to echo inside my head, and I half remembered a boy with dark hair and a thin face offering me a box… I tried to keep a hold on the memory but I couldn't…' All the frustration she felt was there in her sigh.

'And you think that boy was me?'

'Don't *you* know?' Her eyes and voice beseeched him.

'Yes, it was,' he admitted abruptly. 'I gave you a box of Turkish delight on your eighth birthday.'

'Then we *did* know each other as children?'

'Our families were neighbours.'

A thought struck her, and she asked, 'My mother didn't know who you were? Didn't recognise you?'

'She was hardly likely to. I was only thirteen at the time, and she'd known me as Clave.'

'The same as I did.'

'Yes.'

'Were we friends?'

'No. I was five years older than you. That kind of age gap is too wide for friendship, even had we been so inclined. But I remember you as a quiet, skinny little thing, with a mop of dark hair, huge violet eyes and a kind of infuriating self-sufficiency… Even then it was clear you'd grow up to be a beauty. Like your mother.

'We lived just outside Meredith, at Foxton Priory. Your family lived at Stratton Place, about a quarter of a

mile away. As well as neighbours, our families were good friends—' his voice now held a glacial coldness '—your mother and mine were particularly close...'

Clare began to shiver, chilled by a sudden nameless dread, a premonition of disaster.

Jos looked at her, his gaze hard and inimical, and at that moment she knew he was seeing her mother's face rather than her own.

Through stiff lips, she asked, 'What happened? What did my mother do?'

He answered slowly, 'She was my father's lover and the direct cause of my own mother committing suicide...'

'Suicide?' Clare whispered, aghast. This was worse than anything she might have envisaged.

Jos drew a harsh breath. 'Though somehow they managed to hush things up and get a verdict of accidental death, I knew it was suicide. She hadn't been able to bear to lose the man she'd devoted all her adult life to.'

While one part of Clare's mind struggled to take in the implications, another part remained curiously detached, isolated from the shock and horror.

She heard the faint, musical splash of the fountain on the terrace, and through the open window smelt the tubs of night-scented stock. The curtains hadn't been closed, and beyond the trees in Central Park she saw that the squares and rectangles of the lighted windows of Upper West Side formed geometrical patterns against the dark buildings.

'Your mother betrayed and caused the death of the woman who was her best friend.' Jos's biting accusation broke the lengthening silence. 'But though she shed tears at the funeral, and said how sorry she was, she never appeared to feel any real guilt or shame...'

No! No! Clare cried silently. She couldn't believe it.

Some instinct insisted that though her mother might have been weak, she hadn't been *wicked*.

But with her memory gone, how could she be sure?

Clutching at straws, Clare asked, scarcely above a whisper, 'Was she *truly* so cruel and heartless?'

As though striving to be fair, Jos answered evenly, 'When she set out to seduce my father I don't suppose she anticipated quite such tragic results.'

'You seem to be laying all the responsibility at her door... Remember it takes two to tango.'

'Reduced to quoting clichés?' he sneered, apparently angered by her attempt to defend the indefensible.

'It may be a cliché, but like most clichés it contains more than a grain of truth.'

Irritably, he said, 'I'm not trying to pretend my father was entirely blameless, but if Isobel had set out to seduce the Archangel Gabriel he would have had a struggle to resist her...'

In her mind Clare heard the echo of Jos's earlier words, 'I knew only too well how immoral and unscrupulous she was, but I still had to fight the pull of her physical attraction...'

Trying desperately to find some small excuse, some shred of evidence in mitigation, Clare found herself asking, 'You don't think they...my mother and your father...might have loved each other?'

Flatly, he answered, 'I very much doubt it. If they were in love it didn't survive my mother's death...at least not on Isobel's side. Immediately afterwards she dropped him, and he started drinking heavily. So you see, she was also, indirectly, the cause of *his* death.'

CHAPTER EIGHT

'IT SEEMS she had a great deal to answer for,' Clare said quietly.

'Indeed she had, but it wasn't until after he was dead and buried that she showed the slightest trace of remorse...'

Remorse... Written in letters of fire, the word seemed to be burning into her brain. *Remorse...* With a little half-stifled moan she closed her eyes, trying to shut out the pain, but it was still there inside her head and she moaned again.

Gripping her upper arms, Jos demanded, 'What is it? What can you remember?'

His obvious concern, his urgency got through, and after a moment she pulled herself together and answered a shade unsteadily, 'Nothing really. It was just that word...' As he released his grip she went on, 'You once said it would spoil all your plans if I didn't remember. What did you mean, exactly?'

For an instant he seemed discomposed, then he said evenly, 'What do you think I meant?'

She drew a deep breath and, applying her new-found knowledge, said, 'I think you meant that for you to enjoy your revenge to the full I would need to remember *why* you married me, need to remember what I was being punished for.'

'You think I married you to punish you for your mother's sins?'

'Didn't you?'

He turned his head to look at her. 'It was rather more complicated than that.'

Her mouth dry, she asked, 'Before I lost my memory, had you meant to tell me the truth?'

'Yes, but not straight away.'

'Didn't it occur to you that when you did I might leave you?'

'I judged you would have enough spirit to stay.'

'You must have thought I was some kind of masochist.'

His bare shoulders moved in a slight shrug. 'There would still have been the things you'd married me for. Wealth. Lifestyle. The way our tastes and minds are in accord... And, as I mentioned previously, the bonds of passion to tie you to me... But before those bonds were in place—'

'I ran away and got knocked down by a cab. Why did I go?'

'Our full names were used during the marriage service, and you realised, rather belatedly, who I was...'

And even though she couldn't have known the whole story, Clare thought, it must have come as a shock, made her wonder why he'd kept his true identity a secret.

With sudden clarity she recalled the two snapshots he had shown her. In the first, taken on the day they'd become engaged, she had been happy and smiling, a woman in love.

In the second, taken after their wedding, there had been no smile on her face and she'd looked tense and nervous.

'During the journey back to the States,' Jos went on, 'you were very quiet and withdrawn. In the lift on the way up to the apartment you remarked that you were scared of heights—'

'Just as I did that night you brought me home from hospital. And both times you said, "Then perhaps you shouldn't have chosen to marry a man who lives in a penthouse"...'

'How do you know?' Jos demanded sharply.

'I had a feeling of *déjà vu*—only I realise now the feeling wasn't illusory. Please go on...'

'Well, after that, you seemed even more uneasy, and while we ate supper and Roberts unpacked you asked me point-blank why I'd married you...'

'And you told me the truth?'

'Some of it. Too much, apparently. You refused to sleep with me, said you needed time to think things over. It was late and you were very tired. There seemed no point in forcing the issue just then, so I slept in the guest room.

'Next morning I was forced to go into the office, just briefly. I'd been in England for quite a while, and they needed my signature on some papers. You appeared to be still asleep, so I didn't waken you.

'When I got home I found you'd gone. I must confess I hadn't expected such a violent reaction. It took me completely by surprise...'

Well, it would have, because he'd got his calculations all wrong. She hadn't married him for any of the reasons he'd listed. And the thing she *had* married him for was the one thing that must have made her unable to stay.

'I knew you hadn't taken your passport—as luck would have it I'd slipped both passports into the pocket of the jacket I was wearing—so you couldn't leave the States. Nor had you taken any clothes. That meant one of two things: either you intended to come back, or you'd been afraid to stay and pack.

'You hadn't any dollars, or much English money, so

if your idea had been to lie low for a while, I couldn't understand why you'd left valuable rings behind...'

She could, Clare thought trenchantly.

'Though I was very glad you had—for more than one reason.'

As though recalling that morning was a far from pleasant experience, Jos's jaw tightened. 'I wasn't sure what to do for the best. New York can be a dangerous place if you don't know which areas to avoid...'

'I wasn't sure what to do for the best...' Assured, assertive, self-confident Jos? It was so out of character that Clare was staggered.

Like someone in a dream, she found herself asking, 'What did you do?'

'I called a top private detective agency and hired all the good people they could spare. Within an hour they were out, armed with photographs of you, making enquiries, checking guest houses and hotels... But it was a mammoth task...

'Of course, there was still a chance that you'd return of your own accord, but I didn't want to lose any time. All I could think of was getting you back safely and as soon as possible...

'When evening came, and they'd drawn a blank, I started to ring round the hospitals—there are more than one hundred and fifty in New York City—all the while terrified of what I might discover...' His face was rigid, his lean body taut as a drawn bowstring.

A tremor running through her, she realised that though he might not love her, his feelings for her had a dark depth she had never envisaged.

Trying for casualness, she observed, 'So it must have come as a relief when you found out I'd only had a trifling accident.'

'If you'd cracked your skull,' he said grimly, 'that "trifling accident" could have been fatal...'

In a sense it *had* been fatal. Losing her memory had put her back in his power, given him a chance to form those bonds of passion he had talked about.

'And if anything had happened to you...' His voice was harsh, ragged, full of raw emotion.

Putting out his hand, he touched her cheek. There was something fiercely possessive in the gesture, but nothing of the tenderness she yearned for. His index finger traced the line of her lips before moving to find a linger on the pulse hammering away at the base of her throat.

'That first day I saw you in Ashleigh Kent's office, I couldn't take my eyes off you. You were so beautiful, so—'

'Like my mother?' she interrupted jerkily.

When he didn't answer, she said in a strangled voice, 'And because I *looked* like her, you thought I *was* like her.'

'Yes, for a while.' He drew back with a sigh. 'But nothing seemed to add up properly. So many things didn't fit.'

'I wonder why I didn't recognise you.'

'Seventeen years is a long time.'

'Did we meet entirely by chance?' Even as she asked she knew that that would have been too much of a co-incidence.

'No.'

'You knew I worked there?'

'Isobel mentioned it.' Abruptly, he added, 'Though she said for the most part you'd lived separate lives, she seemed fond of you.'

A little warmth crept into Clare's cold heart, only to be immediately frozen over. 'Then your "business trip" was made simply to get to know me?'

'If necessary I would have made the trip solely for that purpose, but, to use a hackneyed phrase, fortune took a hand…'

He sounded relaxed now, self-assured, once more master of himself and his emotions.

'I'd been notified that a house I was interested in buying had come on the market. The sale was being handled by Ashleigh Kent. That simplified matters and enabled me to kill two birds with one stone. All I had to do was tell them I was looking for a property and ask for you to show me round.'

'And the rest was easy,' she said with some bitterness.

'Not as easy as I'd envisaged,' he corrected smoothly. 'Though you didn't seem to remember me on any conscious level, I sometimes wondered if your subconscious knew me. I could tell you had an interest in me as a man, as well as in my money, but you were so cool, so wary, I was forced to move very carefully…'

A chill ran through her as she recalled her own half-formed suspicion that he'd *stalked* her…

'How soon did you decide to marry me?'

'That very first day. I wanted you the moment I set eyes on you.'

So the bitter, unwilling sexual attraction he'd felt for her mother had been transferred to herself, along with his unsatisfied desire for revenge.

Hotly, she said, 'Then I was right the first time. I *am* just a stand-in for my mother.'

'I've already told you, you're no such thing.'

Ignoring his curt denial, she rushed on, 'You just see me as a body you can use to get rid of urges you despise and want to be purged of because fate got in first and you lost the chance to take your revenge, as a scapegoat to be punished for my mother's sins.'

'That might have been so originally,' he admitted.

'Now it's no longer the case. My views have started to change. I can even feel a kind of sneaking pity for *her*, for what she became…'

'I don't believe you!'

She *knew* he was lying. He hated her mother, held her responsible for the loss of his home and his parents, and for his subsequent years of misery,

But had it been all Isobel's fault?

There were two sides to everything, and until she got her memory back there was no real way of knowing whether so much hatred was justified.

Until she got her memory back… *If* she got her memory back… And what would she do if she didn't?

Living in a world of shadows and half-truths, knowing he would never feel any warmth or affection for her, her spirit trapped in the shell of an empty mind, her body trapped in the gilded cage of an empty marriage, she would eventually be destroyed, her heart and her spirit broken. That might sound melodramatic, but nevertheless it was so…

'I can't bear it!' she choked despairingly. 'You've got to let me go.'

Suddenly she was crying, hot tears rolling down her cheeks in a steady, silent stream. She turned her head away, pressing her lips tightly together, trying not to make a sound, trying to stem the flow.

But he saw, and said gently, 'Don't cry, my love.'

The endearment was her undoing. It opened the floodgates, releasing all the tensions of the past weeks. She began to sob, harsh, gasping sobs that hurt her throat and took more breath than she'd got.

Jos drew her close, one hand cradling her head against his chest, the other moving up and down her spine in a curiously soothing gesture until she began to quieten and the sobs died away.

When she was all cried out, he slid down the bed, taking her with him. Switching out the light, he settled her head against his shoulder and held her until she slept.

Clare awoke to bright sunlight and a feeling almost of well-being. As she sighed and stretched remembrance came swiftly. Just as swiftly the feeling of well-being vanished.

A quick glance showed the other side of the bed was empty, and the faint sound of running water told her Jos was in the shower.

She shivered. Since the night he had picked her up from the hospital she had been sure there was something dark and bitter in their relationship. Now, thanks to Andrea's jealousy, she knew what it was…

And it was worse than anything she might have suspected. She couldn't, *wouldn't* stay to become a whipping-boy. If he refused to let her go freely, at the first opportunity she would retrieve her passport and fly back to England, even if it meant selling her rings.

Once there, if she chose a big enough city, it should be easy to disappear without trace. She could find a bedsitter, a job of some kind, start a new life. She would never have to set eyes on Jos again…

At the thought of never seeing him again she felt as though she was being shut in an iron maiden. Yet she couldn't stay with him; it would be too hard, too cruelly painful.

Loving him as she did, knowing how he felt about her would be more than she could bear. Her mind would be always in a turmoil…

But what about Jos?

All at once she felt deeply ashamed. How blindly selfish to be thinking only of herself. Her mother, however unintentionally, had wrecked his life, made him the kind of man he was.

A man who used women and despised them, who lived in a luxurious prison rather than a home. A man who had grown up to be hard and bitter and was, in spite of all his wealth, *lonely*.

He had always been alone, and if she left him now, unable to give love or receive it, he was likely to remain alone—except for women like Andrea, who believed he had no needs apart from purely sexual ones.

But surely he needed other things as well? Warmth, laughter, companionship, that rapport of minds and tastes he'd talked about...? All things she could give him.

She was sure that he wanted her, and if he also wanted some kind of retribution then she couldn't find it in her heart to blame him. Surely she owed him that much?

If she stayed freely, willingly, without him having to force her, if she gave him all she had to give, including love, surely her mind would be at rest?

Andrea had said he wouldn't want her love, and, re-membering his own comments on the subject, Clare had no doubt that the blonde was right. But it would be her secret gift to him, her way of making reparation for the harm her mother had done...

'Awake?'

Clare jumped. She had been so deep in thought she hadn't heard him emerge from the bathroom, and now he was standing by the bed looking down at her.

Her pulse began to race with alarming speed, and she felt a heated surge of desire.

He was naked apart from a white towel slung around his neck, and his hair was still damp and mussed from its towelling. Freshly shaved, his olive skin clear and healthy, fuzzed on the chest and arms by a light sprinkling of crisp body hair, his green eyes brilliant between thick dark lashes, he looked disturbingly virile and attractive.

Perhaps something of what she was thinking showed in her face, because he said, 'If you look at me like that I might be tempted to come back to bed, and I dare say you wouldn't like that.'

'You'd be wrong,' she said boldly.

He raised a dark winged brow. 'Well, well, well...'

To her annoyance, Clare felt herself starting to blush.

Sitting on the edge of the bed, his eyes ironic, he watched the colour mount in her cheeks. 'Is this sudden compliance...enthusiasm...whichever...designed to put me off my guard?'

'I don't know what you mean,' she said stiffly.

'I mean are you planning to run off again the minute I turn my back?'

'No.' Taking a deep breath, she announced firmly, 'I have every intention of staying.'

'For how long?'

'For as long as you want me.'

He looked at her thoughtfully. 'Does that mean you've changed your mind about not believing me?'

As she hesitated he said incisively, 'No, I can see you haven't.' Then, with that lightning perception that was so unnerving, he went on, 'So you've decided you owe me something and you're going to make reparation? Well, isn't that nice?'

She hadn't been prepared for such a sardonic reaction, and, infuriated by his open mockery, she cried fiercely, 'Oh, go to hell!'

Green eyes gleaming, he clicked his tongue reprovingly. 'If you're planning to be a tractable wife, that's no way to speak to your husband.'

She fought back. 'I don't recall saying I was going to be *tractable*.'

'That's just as well. Too much docility would bore me. I'd much prefer you to be fiery and passionate, maybe even a little rebellious at times...'

'So you can have the fun of taming me?'

He laughed, showing white, even teeth. 'How did you guess?'

With an air of calm deliberation, he tossed the towel aside, drew back the lightweight duvet and got in beside her.

Repressing an instinctive urge to move away from so much overpowering maleness, she made herself lie quite still while he propped himself up on one elbow and smiled down into her wary violet eyes.

'Well?'

'Well, what?' she snapped, flustered by his manner.

'Now you've enticed me back to bed, what are you going to do with me?'

Her heart sank. Plainly he was out to tease and taunt her.

When she didn't answer, he sighed theatrically. 'Surely you can think of something to...shall we say amuse me?'

His smile was devilish, derisory, and her insides knotted with tension as she realised that beneath his cool veneer of lazy mockery he was furiously angry with her.

The last trace of desire fled with the realisation, leaving her feeling chilled and frightened.

But why was he so furious? Had she hurt his pride in some way? Did he think she was presuming to offer him pity? Or was he angry that she hadn't believed his assurance that he no longer wanted to punish her for her mother's sins?

'Jos, I...' She faltered to a halt.

'Perhaps you could begin by kissing me?' he suggested blandly. 'And see what that leads to?'

'I haven't cleaned my teeth,' she muttered, 'and I need a shower.'

'Chickening out?' he queried, interestedly.

'No, I'm not,' she snarled.

'Then I'll wait.'

Scrambling out of the opposite side of the bed, she grabbed her satin robe and fled into the bathroom.

Having showered, cleaned her teeth and brushed her shoulder-length dark hair, she pulled on her robe and stood irresolute. Could she bring herself to go back and face his biting scorn and fury?

But it wasn't a case of whether she *could* or not; really she had no choice.

Perhaps if she waited a while he might get impatient and come and fetch her. It would make things so much easier if *he* took the initiative.

Even as the thought crossed her mind she knew that he wouldn't. He was a ruthless, sadistic devil, and he had no intention of making things easier for her.

So was she going to let him rout her completely?

Was she hell!

Squaring her shoulders, she tightened her belt and headed for the door. Her hand was on the knob when she paused... Making up her mind, she untied the belt, discarded the robe, and with the light of battle in her eyes sallied forth.

He was lying on top of the duvet now, stretched full-length, relaxed and indolent, eyes closed, hands clasped behind his dark head.

Though he must have known she'd returned he kept his eyes closed, obviously waiting for her to make the first move.

Well, she would surprise him by doing just that, by

taking the initiative. Nerving herself, she stretched out beside him and, propped on one elbow, studied his face.

His hair was rumpled and his mocking eyes hidden. The closed lids and long dark lashes lying on his hard cheekbones gave him a boyish, vulnerable look.

Her resentment faded, leaving only love. The intention to boldly caress and arouse him forgotten, with a little murmur of tenderness, she leaned over to kiss his cheek.

At the touch of her lips his eyes flew open, and with a smothered oath he pushed her roughly away and leapt out of bed.

'Jos, what is it?' she whispered. 'What's the matter?'

'You can save the play-acting,' he told her savagely. 'It's enough to have you in my bed. I don't need any pretence of love.'

A second later the door into the dressing room slammed behind him.

Staring at the white panels, her eyes filled with stinging tears.

She had set out to make him lose his calm, and had succeeded in a way she had never envisaged.

Over the next two or three weeks, while the heatwave continued unrelentingly, Jos took her out and about, showing her New York from the Bronx to Battery Park.

The city was hot and airless and dusty, but Clare found she loved the thrill and excitement of the place, and the supposition, not to say conviction of most native New Yorkers that it was the hub of the universe.

Together, almost making a game of it, they did all the touristy things. They visited SoHo and Chinatown, crossed Brooklyn Bridge, climbed the Statue of Liberty and went to the top of the great pointing needle of the Empire State Building.

Making an effort at least to come to terms with her

fear of heights, Clare had gritted her teeth and forced herself to tackle the latter two.

Climbing the spiralling metal stairway up to Liberty's crown had been just bearable so long as she didn't look down. But in the Empire State lift her ears had popped uncomfortably, making her wonder if she would ever get used to New York skyscrapers. And when they'd reached the top she'd found herself trembling, gripped by a kind of nausea, and had been only too pleased to have the comfort of Jos's arm around her.

Though she still couldn't think of the penthouse as home, she became more used to it, and was quite happy on the terrace so long as she kept away from the balustrade.

As if by tacit consent they never talked about the past or Clare's loss of memory, but sometimes she caught him looking at her oddly, and one day, when she'd asked him why, he'd said, 'You still have that lost look... I thought it might go away, but it hasn't.'

In the evenings they went out to dine and dance in the top nightspots, to shows and concerts and sometimes, though less frequently after she admitted how much it bothered her, to parties to meet more of his friends and acquaintances.

For the most part they were nice people, whom she felt she should have been comfortable with, but her memory loss made her sensitive to casual queries, such as, 'What a beautiful ring! Where did Jos take you to buy it?'

That time she'd stammered, 'Well, I—I...'

Squeezing her hand, smiling down at her, Jos had responded quickly. 'We got it in London's Bond Street, didn't we, darling?'

And though he made a point of never leaving her side, and was always ready to field any awkward questions, she felt foolish and embarrassed when he had to answer for her.

'I almost feel I could cope better with some physical disability,' she'd said to Jos late one night. 'At least that would be visible, something people could see and accept without needing explanations. As it is, I'm frightened to even try and explain in case they think I'm...well...not all there.'

'No one would think that,' he'd said brusquely.

'Andrea did.'

'Andrea didn't. She was just being bitchy.'

To Clare's great relief they'd seen nothing more of the blonde, and until that moment neither of them had referred to that traumatic evening.

Though, at times, the thought of it made her shiver, she never for an instant regretted her decision to stay with Jos. He was everything, and more, that she could have dared hope for, and every day she fell steadily deeper in love.

With him she found a kind of poignant, bittersweet pleasure, an ephemeral happiness that left her only too aware that any lasting happiness and contentment depended on two things: Jos loving her enough to want *her* love, and her getting her memory back.

Both seemed unattainable.

Yet just being with him was precious to her, and each day she found herself eagerly looking forward to all the pleasures the nights brought: going to bed together hand in hand, making love—slow, delectable love, fierce, passionate love—sometimes just lying quietly in his arms while they talked over their day.

It was a serene interlude, a time of peace, yet a peace that was oddly fragile, as if they were waiting for some kind of explosion that they both sensed was inevitable.

Towards the end of the third week, it came.

They were just finishing breakfast on the terrace when Roberts carried out the morning post. Amongst the small pile of envelopes were two letters that bore English stamps.

Jos tore open the first, and as he glanced through it Clare caught a look of blazing excitement and triumph. It was gone almost immediately, leaving his green eyes cool, his face expressionless.

The second, from a firm of solicitors, was addressed to *Mrs* J. Saunders. Jos passed it to her, and with a strange feeling of trepidation that amounted almost to foreboding, Clare unfolded the single sheet of headed paper and read it.

Dear Mrs Saunders,

As you are aware, we act in the administration of the estate of Sir Roger and Lady Isobel Berkeley. In furtherance of this we should be grateful if you would advise us as soon as possible if you still wish to proceed with the sale of Stratton Place, willed to you by your late parents.

Ashleigh Kent, the estate agents you nominated, now have several parties interested. Though, as we pointed out before you left for the United States, the property market is still somewhat depressed, the proceeds from the sale of the house and contents, should you wish to part with them, should prove adequate to clear any outstanding debts.

We await your instructions.

Yours sincerely,

YORK, THOMAS & WILDGOOSE

Clare looked up to find Jos watching her intently. Without a word she handed him the letter.

When he'd read it, she asked, 'Did you know about the house?'

'Yes, I knew.' His green eyes hooded, he queried carefully, 'So what do you intend to do?'

Heart thumping, she asked, 'What do you think I should do?'

As though he knew what half-formed thought lay behind her question, he answered indirectly, 'I have to go to England myself soon.'

'And you think I should go with you?'

'I think you should make up your own mind.'

'The very idea makes me feel on-edge and nervous,' she admitted.

'You could be taking a risk, disturbing the status quo. It depends, surely, on how much you want your memory back.'

She sighed. 'I can't *tell* you how much. There's only one thing in the world I want more.' The fateful words were out before she could prevent them.

His face growing suddenly taut, he asked, 'And what might that be?'

Flushing hotly, knowing she couldn't bring herself to sit and beg for love he was incapable of giving her, she stammered, 'W-well, I—'

'There's no need to tell me,' he interrupted, his voice curt. 'I can guess. You'd like your freedom and a substantial divorce settlement.'

As, startled, she began to shake her head he went on grimly, 'Well, I've no intention of giving you either.'

Before she could try to undo the damage her unthinking stupidity had caused, he rose to his feet, tall and dark, icily composed. 'If getting your memory back means that much to you, then I think you *should* go to England.' Tossing down his napkin, he headed for the sliding glass doors.

'Jos, please wait…I need to talk to you.'

'We can talk later.'

'But where are you going?'

'I've some things to do, some arrangements to make. Then I propose to go into the office.'

'How long will you be gone?'

'I don't know. Most of the day, probably.'

He left without another word, and without kissing her. Sitting at the table, Clare had to struggle to hold back her tears.

CHAPTER NINE

WITHOUT JOS, the morning dragged endlessly, the book she was trying to read completely failing to hold her attention.

As though to match her mood, the weather was breaking up, becoming gloomy and overcast, with heavy spots of rain plopping onto the terrace and rumbles of thunder in the distance.

Having resisted Roberts' efforts to serve lunch in the dining room, Clare ate a solitary salad in the kitchen which, in spite of all its shining gadgetry, seemed to her to be the most homely room in the apartment.

Lunch over, a glance at her watch showed it was barely one o'clock. With a sinking heart, she realised that the afternoon threatened to drag even more than the morning had.

Rebelling against the boredom, deciding to pass some time by going down to the foyer and having a wander round the shops, Clare collected her shoulder-bag and donned a light jacket.

Roberts was hovering in the hall looking somewhat uncomfortable. 'Madam wasn't planning to go out? A thunderstorm appears to be imminent.'

'I'm not afraid of storms,' she said briskly, and wondered how she could be so sure. 'And anyway, I'm not actually going *out*. I'm just planning to do a spot of window-shopping.'

Looking even more uncomfortable, the manservant

observed, 'Mr Saunders was most anxious that after what happened last time madam shouldn't venture anywhere alone.'

Clare bit her lip. Clearly Roberts had received instructions not to let her go out. But what if she insisted? Had he been ordered to restrain her physically?

He was a nice man, and, unwilling to put them both in an embarrassing situation, she decided not to risk it.

Lightly, she said, 'In that case, though I'm quite sure Mr Saunders is fussing unnecessarily, I'll wait until he gets home.' And she watched the relief spread across the manservant's usually impassive face.

Taking off the jacket, she handed it to him, and then, feeling frustrated and rebellious, asked on a sudden impulse, 'Roberts, do you know how to play poker?'

If he was surprised, he hid it well, merely answering, 'Yes, madam.'

'Have we got any cards in the house?'

'I believe so, madam.'

'Then perhaps you'd be kind enough to bring them to the kitchen and teach me how to play poker.'

'The *kitchen*, madam?' He seemed more distressed by the location than any other consideration.

'The kitchen,' she said firmly. 'Oh, and Roberts, have we any bourbon?'

'Would madam not prefer a little wine, perhaps?'

Shaking her head, she said seriously, 'Bourbon seems much more appropriate.'

She was sitting at the kitchen table waiting when the manservant appeared with a new pack of cards, a bottle of bourbon and two small bags of what looked remarkably like dried beans.

Having opened the whisky, he produced a tray of ice cubes and a single glass.

'You drink bourbon, don't you?' Clare queried.

'Indeed, madam, but not during working hours.'

'Then you'd better have the afternoon off. I can't drink alone... Now, just run through the game for me...'

When the manservant had carefully explained the intricacies of poker, she said, 'Yes, I'm sure I must have played it. Let's make a start and see how I get on...' Then she asked curiously, 'Roberts, what are the beans for?'

'I thought madam might wish to place a bet...'

The evening finally brought the threatened storm, but there was still no sign of Jos. After asking Roberts to delay dinner for more than an hour, and getting angrier by the minute, Clare had finally eaten alone and then gone straight to bed.

If Jos thought he could treat her like this, walking out and leaving her a virtual prisoner, then he had another think coming!

But where *was* he? It didn't seem feasible that he would still be working. She pushed away a sudden mental picture of Andrea's cold blonde beauty. No, she couldn't believe he was with another woman.

Or was it just that she didn't *want* to believe it?

Her anger was turning to a sick fear that something must have happened to him when finally, lying in the dark, awake and unsettled, Clare heard his voice as he spoke to Roberts and then, a short time later, the click of the bedroom door.

Without putting on the light, he crossed to the bathroom, and a few seconds later she heard the shower running.

When finally he emerged and, still without speaking, got into bed beside her and turned his broad back, she could have wept with frustration.

Too uptight to try and sleep, and determined to have

things out, she pushed herself up and reached to switch on her bedside lamp, bathing them both in a pool of light.

Her voice carefully moderated, she said, 'I'd like to talk to you.'

He turned to look at her, pushing himself up on one elbow, tension etched sharply on his dark face. Coldly, he informed her, 'I'm in no mood to talk. I've had a long, frustrating day.'

Her breathing quickening to match her temper, she threw caution to the winds and said, just as coldly, 'So have I. That's one of the things I want to talk to you about. As you're so fond of telling me, I *chose* to marry you. Even after I discovered why you married me, I *chose* to stay with you, and I *intend* to stay with you. I don't want a divorce and I don't want your money.'

His expression was shuttered and it was impossible to tell whether or not he believed her.

'But I *do* want some freedom. Don't think you can just stalk out and stay out, and then keep me here like a prisoner.'

When he remained silent, merely looking at her with glittering green eyes, her anger boiled over. 'I refuse to be treated like something of no consequence—a…a sex-object with no will of my own. I *won't* just be used whenever it suits you…'

The words ended in a throaty gasp as he rolled over, pinning her beneath him. With a kind of raging calm, he said, 'You'll be treated exactly as I want to treat you, used whenever I want to use you…'

She began to struggle then, striking out at him, wanting to hurt him. But with a cruel disregard for her feelings as a woman he used his superior strength to force her to compliance, and for the first time took her brutally, without any preliminaries.

She should have been scared by the violence she'd aroused, but her anger rose to meet and match his, and in that instant it changed to a searing, white-hot passion that sent them both up in flames.

He was kissing her mouth now, and his hands were beneath her buttocks, lifting her. She felt intense pleasure, a fierce concentration that wasn't just physical but emotional, a longing for release, a desperate wish for his love.

Her release came with a brilliant flash of light, an explosion of ecstasy that sent her mind reeling and made her cry out again and again.

The weight of his dark head against her breast was a pleasurable burden while their breathing and heartbeats slowed to a more normal rate.

It wasn't until he lifted his head and said with sudden urgency, 'Don't cry… For God's sake don't cry…' that she realised tears were running down her cheeks.

'I'm sorry.' He sounded anguished. 'I didn't mean to hurt you.'

'You didn't hurt me,' she assured him as he brushed the tears away with his fingertips. 'It was *wonderful*.' Smiling at him, hearing his indrawn breath of relief, she added with a throaty chuckle, 'Perhaps I should make you angry more often…'

Observing sternly, 'Perhaps you shouldn't push your luck,' he reached to switch off the light, and, stretching out beside her, pulled her close against him so that her head was on his shoulder, her body half supported by his.

'Jos…' She had to ask. 'Where have you been all evening?'

'You're beginning to sound like a wife.'

'Of course, if you don't want to tell me…'

He sighed. 'Earlier I went to talk to Dr Hauser about

your amnesia. He suggested that I got in touch with a Paul Gregson, who's a specialist in the field. After an afternoon spent trying, I finally tracked Gregson down at a West Side clinic. He already had an early evening appointment, so I invited him to dine with me later...'

'And?'

'He wasn't a great deal of help. All he would say was that amnesia can sometimes be a functional disturbance of the nervous system—a defence mechanism, if you like.

'I asked if remembering anything unpleasant could harm you. He hedged a bit, and then said that so long as you *want* to remember, you'll probably be able to cope if and when you do.'

Jos sounded anxious, dissatisfied, far from reassured. She found herself wondering what unpleasant things he'd omitted to tell her, but knew it was no use asking.

'I'm sure I will,' she said, with more conviction than she felt. Then, nestling against him, she went on, 'It was kind of you to go to all that trouble, but, Jos...' Her fingers traced slow circles in the crisp dark hair on his chest. 'Don't leave me again like that.'

Half humorously, he said, 'I wouldn't dare! I don't know what I might find when I get home. Already you've been leading Roberts astray. Encouraging him to drink and play poker...giving him the afternoon off...and worst of all hurting his feelings.'

'Hurting his feelings?' she echoed.

'He tells me you won all his beans.'

Still oddly restive, unable to sleep, Clare lay for what seemed an age, uneasily aware that Jos was also lying wakeful.

Though on the surface things appeared to be all right between them, she knew that the calm of the preceding few weeks was over. Not only had the letter from the solicitors disturbed their tranquillity, but her unthinking words had torn a rent in the delicate fabric of their almost-happiness that she wasn't certain was mended.

Perhaps her restlessness communicated itself to Jos, because, though it was long past midnight before she finally fell asleep, he was still lying wide awake staring into the darkness.

Next morning, even though it was early when she stirred and opened her eyes, Jos had already showered and breakfasted.

Wearing a smart lightweight suit and silk shirt, he was standing in front of the dressing table knotting his tie. His handsome face looked grim and preoccupied.

Sitting up in bed, Clare met his eyes in the mirror and smiled tentatively at him.

He didn't return her smile.

'You're looking very businesslike,' she remarked, with what lightness she could muster. 'Are you going into the office?'

'Only for ten minutes. I have a couple more things to attend to before we start for JFK.'

'We're flying to England today?'

'Yes. We're booked on Concorde. I'm sorry I didn't get round to telling you last night.'

But she guessed the omission had been a deliberate one, designed to give her less time to worry.

He turned to face her, saying evenly, 'I hope you agree that there's no point in delay, that it's better to get things over with?'

'Yes.' Clare sighed inwardly, finding his cool civility more off-putting than anger.

'We could no doubt get a room at the Barley Mow— that's where I stayed last time—but it might make more sense to stay at Lamb Cottage.'

'That's the cottage I rented?'

'Yes. I understand the leave still has a couple of months to run. You didn't give it up because some of your belongings were being left there until you'd decided whether or not to have them shipped over.'

Pushing back her cloud of dark hair, she asked, 'Do I still have the keys?'

'They were left with Mrs Carter, the lady who lives next door. I gather she's the niece of the man who actually owns it, and she acts as caretaker. I'll get in touch with her and tell her to expect us.'

'You think staying at the cottage might trigger my memory?'

'It's possible.'

His voice was casual, non-committal, but she guessed that he was still worried, far from happy at the prospect.

The flight on the beautiful, graceful plane was smooth and fast and incident-free. Jos appeared withdrawn, deep in thought, and for the greater part of the journey a silence hung between them, sheer and impenetrable as a glass wall.

Formalities over, they got into the hired car that was waiting for them and, leaving the bustle of the airport behind them, drove down to Meredith through quiet county lanes and pleasant, rolling countryside.

They had left the bad weather over the Atlantic, and the evening was calm and slightly hazy. It was just starting to get dusk, and as they approached the outskirts of the old, carefully preserved village Clare could see the bats were out, flittering around the period streetlamps and the lighted sign of the Barley Mow.

Lamb Cottage was one of a row of six rose- and creeper-covered stone cottages facing the village green and duck pond. Though they were joined, each of the roofs had a slightly different pitch and the chimneys were at various angles, giving them a look of slightly rakish individuality. At each end the outer cottages leaned in a little, like amiable drunks supporting their neighbours.

At the end of the little road that fronted them was a neatly paved area, partly screened by trees and bushes, that served as a car park.

Mrs Carter, a plump, round-faced woman with frizzy fair hair, opened her door to Jos's knock, spilling yellow light into the porch, and handed him two bunches of keys. 'I've given you the spare set as well, in case you want one each. The place is aired, I've made up the bed and lit the water-heater, and I've got the groceries you asked for.'

When Jos had thanked her, and given her a smile that visibly melted her, with an effort she transferred her attention to Clare. 'It's nice to see you again, Miss Berkeley...I should say Mrs Saunders. Are you liking New York?'

Breathing in the scent of roses and honeysuckle, Clare smiled at the woman who was a total stranger to her and said, 'Loving it.'

'It must be very different to village life?'

'Yes, it is.'

'I've often wondered what it must be like to live in one of those skyscrapers...'

Mrs Carter seemed set for a long chat, and Clare was wondering how best to cut it short without hurting her feelings when Jos, who had moved away to unlock the door to Lamb Cottage, called, 'Darling, could you make some coffee while I park the car and bring in the cases?'

'Yes, of course,' she agreed thankfully.

'Americans and their coffee!' Mrs Carter exclaimed archly.

Clare smiled, and, having said, 'Well, goodnight, then, and thank you again,' lost no time in escaping.

The two-up, two-down cottage, with its tiny low-ceilinged rooms and chintz-covered furniture, was quite charming but totally unfamiliar.

At the front, casement windows looked out across the green to the old village school, and at the back the kitchen overlooked a picket-fenced garden bright with snapdragons and lupins and hollyhocks.

A cardboard box full of groceries stood on the draining board, and several packing cases took up most of the available floor space.

When she'd found the cafetière and plugged in the kettle, Clare opened the door to the staircase and climbed the narrow, cramped stairs, which creaked at every step.

The front bedroom, with its polished floorboards and black-grated fireplace, its faded rugs and flowered counterpane, was ready for occupation. The back bedroom had at some time been converted into a nicely equipped bathroom and, as Mrs Carter had promised, the pilot light on the water-heater had been lit.

Tired from lack of sleep the previous night and a day spent travelling, Clare was thinking longingly of bed when Jos brought up their cases.

His eyes resting on her thoughtfully, he said, 'I take it nothing looks familiar?'

Realising now why he'd let her walk through the cottage alone, she shook her head. 'No, I might never have been here before.' After a moment, she added with a sigh, 'I don't know about you, but I'm ready for bed.'

'Do you want anything to eat, or perhaps a milky drink before you turn in?' he queried, with that cool, disconcerting politeness that she sensed masked real concern and anxiety.

'I don't think so.'

'Then if you'd like to use the bathroom first while I get a cup of coffee…?'

Clare had been in bed for almost half an hour when Jos finally joined her. Though she had put the light out and tried to sleep she was unable to settle, her mind restless and uneasy.

Lying in the semi-darkness, she found herself thinking about her parents, and the house she had come to England to look at. But if the cottage she'd lived in until just a few weeks ago had failed to spark off any memories, what chance would Strattan Place stand?

At the moment it was just a name to her, and a not very familiar name at that. She had no recollection of what it was like or where it stood…

She turned to look at Jos, who was stretched on his back beside her. His handsome profile appeared aloof and unapproachable, but, suddenly determined to break through the barrier he'd erected, she blew softly on his bare shoulder before resting her cheek there and asking, 'Jos, how well do you know Stratton Place? Did you go there much as a child?'

'Yes.' With a kind of bleak humour, he added, 'I almost got to live there.'

Afraid he was going to leave it at that, she begged quickly, 'Please, darling, won't you tell me about it?'

There was a long silence, as though he was debating the advisability of it, and she was just beginning to think he'd decided against telling her when he said flatly, 'I believe I told you that it wasn't until after my father was dead and buried that your mother showed the slightest trace of remorse…?'

Clare's 'Yes' was just a sigh, a thread of sound.

'Your father, who was an extraordinarily good-looking man, tended to stay in the background and say very little, but I'm certain he must have known the score, because he at least had the grace to look ashamed and harassed…'

Poor Father, Clare found herself thinking. He was the one person no one seemed to have felt any sympathy for, yet he too had been a victim of a sort…

But Jos was going on. 'While my parents' solicitors tried to sort out the unholy mess that had been left, I was staying at Stratton Place. When it became obvious that I would have to be put into care, your mother, apparently in a fit of conscience, suggested that they should give me a permanent home, and your father agreed…'

'Then, why…?'

'They asked you what you thought about having me as a brother, but you shook your head and mumbled, "No, I don't want him here." When they pressed you, you cried, "I don't want him to live with us. I don't want him! I hate him!" It was like being rejected all over again.'

'Dear God,' Clare breathed. 'I see now why that day at Niagara you implied that I used to be a heartless little monster…'

As though she hadn't spoken Jos went on, his voice full of black bitterness, 'I didn't really want to live at Stratton Place, for more than one reason, but my life had been turned upside down and your home and family seemed to be the only familiar things left.'

And because of her even they had been lost to him. Desperately, she said, 'But if I was only eight, surely they shouldn't have taken any notice of me?'

'Well, you were pretty vehement about it—almost distraught. Though in retrospect I have to admit it was my fault you felt as you did.'

'Why was it your fault?'

'Because I hadn't always been nice to you. I thought you were a self-righteous little prig. I disliked your haughtiness, your air of superiority, and during the school holidays, behind our parents' backs, I used to tease you unmercifully, try to make you cry... When I said children were heartless little monsters, I was including myself.'

'Did you succeed in making me cry?' she asked curiously.

'No. You had extraordinary composure for a child of that age. You used to look at me with those huge violet eyes and make me feel ashamed—which, of course, only made me want to persecute you more.'

Clare sighed. 'I sound unbearable.'

'There was one thing in your favour, one thing I admired about you—your spirit. You took everything I handed out without begging or whining, and you never split on me...

'I was beginning, reluctantly, to like and respect you—I bought you that box of Turkish delight as a peace offering—when you did something I thought was cruel and unforgivable...' He hesitated, as though wondering whether to go on.

After a moment, she asked uneasily, 'What did I do that was so terrible?'

'You laughed when my mother died.'

Feeling as though she'd been kicked in the solar-plexus, Clare lay frozen, unwilling to believe it but unable to move or protest.

'When I heard that half-stifled giggle I lost my head. I lashed out and hit you as hard as I could, knocking you down... So, you see, after I'd been so cruel to you, I couldn't blame you for not wanting me for a brother.'

Somehow she found her voice. 'But why...*why* did I laugh when you told me your mother had died?'

There was a pause before he said carefully, 'It was

only later I saw your response for what it was...a young child's shocked, unbelieving, half-hysterical reaction...'

A shadowy image loomed in her mind, wraithlike but insistent. She seemed to be on the brink of understanding, of remembering... But there was something he wasn't telling her, something she needed to know to get the full picture.

'What happened after you'd hit me?' Her voice was hoarse.

'You picked yourself up without a word. Your face had gone absolutely white, and I could see the mark of my fist on your cheek. But even then you didn't cry, and when, some time later, your mother asked about the bruise, you said you'd bumped into a door...'

His words were fairly graphic, but they didn't tell her what she needed to know. She sat up in bed and pressed her fingers to her temples in sudden frustration. The knowledge was hovering there, practically within her grasp.

If only she could *remember*...

'What is it?' Jos sat up to peer at her face in the gloom.

As she strove to catch and hold the elusive image it was suddenly blotted out by a black, almost tangible cloud of fear—fear that made her moan and cover her face with her hands.

Taking her wrists, Jos pulled her hands away, trying to read her expression, demanding, 'What do you remember?'

'Nothing. Nothing! Yet it's all there at the back of my mind... If only I *could* remember I think I'd be able to bear things better...'

Then, as she began to tremble, he said, his voice suddenly sharp with anxiety, 'Don't try too hard. Let it go.'

No, she wanted to face the fear and *know*...

But as though her bold decision had put it to flight the blackness began to recede and the knowledge dispersed with it, leaving only a grey emptiness. She stifled a groan.

Gripping her upper arms, his fingers biting in, Jos demanded, 'Clare, are you all right?'

'Yes… Yes, I'm all right,' she assured him shakily.

But she was more than pleased when instead of letting her go and turning away, as she'd half expected, he settled down with her in his arms and held her closely until sleep finally claimed her.

Next morning she opened her eyes to bright sunshine and a sense of complete disorientation. As she blinked at the strange room Jos appeared in the doorway, with a cup and saucer in one hand and a plate of toast in the other, and, as if she'd shaken a kaleidoscope, yesterday's pattern of events fell into place.

He was dressed in smart but casual trousers and a black cotton polo-necked shirt, his jaw was clean-shaven and his dark hair was brushed smoothly back from his high forehead. Though his expression was studiedly calm, relaxed, she sensed a certain tension in his long, lean body.

She hoped he would kiss her, but he didn't. Stifling her disappointment, she accepted the tea and toast and asked, 'Why are you up and about at the crack of dawn?'

'Crack of dawn, nothing. It's gone ten! I've been into the solicitors on your behalf, and into Ashleigh Kent to pick up the keys to Stratton Place and the Priory.'

'Foxton Priory? Your old home?'

He sat down on the edge of the bed. 'After my parents died it had to be disposed of. As I told you, it had been in the family for generations, and I swore I'd get it back as soon as I had the money.

'When the money was available, however, the new owners didn't want to sell. But they promised to let me know if it was ever put on the market...which they did, some months ago.

'That's when I got in touch with Ashleigh Kent and told them I was coming over to England to buy a house in this area.' He smiled a shade grimly. 'They gave me first option on a couple, one of which was the Priory.'

'Showing you round was something I half remembered that day in Central Park...'

She shivered, suddenly excited and afraid, convinced now that somehow Foxton Priory held the key that would unlock both her memory and the past.

Seeing that uncontrollable shiver, Jos asked soberly, 'Are you sure you still want to go through with it?'

'Yes.' There was no hesitation. 'I have to.'

'Then eat your toast and let's get started.'

Less than half an hour later they turned between stone gateposts topped by miniature unicorns and followed the drive through a pretty walled garden to draw up outside Foxton Priory, a charming, seventeenth-century manor-house built in honey-coloured stone.

To the best of her knowledge Clare had never seen it before in her life. Shaking her head at Jos's questioning glance, she commented, 'It's smaller than I'd expected.'

'There's a living-room, a morning-room, a library, a dining-room, a kitchen and six bedrooms. The others have been made into bathrooms.'

'It looks empty,' she observed.

'It is. The previous owners have gone abroad to live.'

She wrinkled her brow. 'I'm surprised the estate agents didn't feel they should send someone with us.'

'That's no longer necessary. I own it. I received confirmation the same day you heard from your solicitors.'

Yes, she could visualise his look of fierce satisfaction and triumph as he'd read the letter. Clearly having it back meant a great deal to him.

Recalling other things—his mention of sweeping changes, his assertion that he'd never considered the penthouse home—she asked slowly, 'Do you intend to live in it?'

'That was my original intention, but now it's up to you.'

Why was it up to her? she wondered.

But all at once she *knew*. Though the house nestled and slept innocent as a babe in the sunshine, there must be something about it that Jos knew would frighten and upset her. Black memories of something that had happened there in the past.

Jumping out of the car, Jos came round to help her out. His hand beneath her elbow, they crossed the old flagstone paving and walked over to the black-studded door. While he produced a heavy bunch of keys and opened both the ordinary and the security locks, Clare held her breath.

The door swung open and, still holding her breath, she walked into a long, wood-panelled hall with a graceful horseshoe staircase rising to the second floor. Despite the dark panelling, polished oak floorboards and double windows at each end gave an overall impression of lightness.

She had no recollection of ever having been here before, and if the house had any bad memories for her they were certainly not apparent. The atmosphere felt calm and friendly; it was impossible to believe that any traces of past unhappiness still lingered here.

Releasing her breath in a sigh, she smiled shakily at Jos who, his face studiously blank, was watching her.

'All right?' he queried.

Relief and frustration mingling, she said, 'I don't recognise it, and it's not at all what I...at least my *subconscious*...expected.'

'What did you subconscious expect?'

'I'm not sure... Something frightening...'

As they walked through the big, sunny, empty rooms Clare's impression of it as a beautiful, tranquil house strengthened. Though it had been altered and modernised, it still kept a feeling of rightness, a harmonious blend of past and present.

No wonder Jos loved it and had wanted it back so much. Though as a child he'd found little real happiness here himself, it seemed to be a house made for fun and laughter, for a big, happy family.

The thought was an oddly poignant one.

When they'd completed their tour, without a word Jos locked up and led the way back to the car.

When they were both seated, their safety belts fastened, he glanced at his watch, and with a frown drawing his dark brows together suggested, 'As it's almost lunchtime, suppose we leave Stratton Place until this afternoon?'

But, all psyched up, Clare said, 'No, I'd rather go now, if you don't mind.'

After a marked hesitation, Jos shrugged and agreed, 'Very well.'

She found herself wondering at his strange reluctance. If it was simply that he was hungry, why hadn't he said so?

Stratton Place was less than half a mile to the east. It was a stone-built three-storey house, much older than she'd envisaged—late sixteenth century, perhaps—with a shallow flight of steps leading up to a porticoed entrance.

Jos drew up on the gravel by the steps and came round to help Clare out.

So this was her childhood home. She had no recollection of living here, yet it seemed vaguely familiar, like something she might have glimpsed in a magazine.

The house lay in a dip, with the lower rooms looking out onto lawns and gardens and high beech hedges, but she guessed that the upper rooms would have marvellous views over the surrounding countryside.

Standing to one side of the steps, she stared up at the house. Though small by country house standards, it was larger than she'd expected. At one time the rooms on the top floor would no doubt have been used as servants' quarters. Now they were probably attics. From a purely practical point of view, she found herself hoping that they weren't full of accumulated junk.

Having produced another large bunch of keys and opened the door, Jos stood quietly to one side, making no effort to hurry her.

Fairly sure now that she was to be disappointed, her memory, that essential part of herself, to be locked away for ever, she mounted the steps and pushed open the door.

CHAPTER TEN

CLARE found herself looking at a rectangular hall of un-
usual design. It was high and white, soaring to open
rafters. On each side a curving staircase led up to two
dark-oak galleries which ran round three sides of the
hall.

On both upper and lower galleries were doors leading
off to various rooms. High, narrow windows, set in the
end wall of the upper gallery, threw lozenges of light
onto the dusty stone flags three floors below.

As she looked up everything whirled hideously round
her head, and icy cold all over, assailed by a sudden
nausea, Clare covered her face with her hands. But, as
though some old, silent film were being run in slow mo-
tion, she saw in her mind's eye a woman, tall and slim
and dark-haired, hurry from one of the doors on the upper balcony, stumble against the balustrade and fall, her
body hitting the flags with a sickening thud. There was
a roaring in her ears, and a second later the scene was
blotted out by a merciful blackness...

When Clare regained consciousness she was slumped
in the passenger seat of the car, and with the door wide
open Jos was crouching beside her, chafing her cold
hands.

Lifting her head, which felt too heavy for her slender
neck, she looked at him, and, her voice sounding oddly
thin and high, like the voice of someone who had been

very ill for a longer time, said, 'We'd been told to stay in the playroom that day, but you complained it was too much like a nursery. We were in the hall together when your mother fell. That was when you hit me...'

He gripped her hands hard. 'Don't try and remember any more.'

'I don't need to *try*.' Seeing the tension, the barely hidden fear on his face, she added, more hardily, 'It's all right, really. Nothing could be worse than not knowing...'

Lifting her hands to his lips, he saluted her courage. 'Do you feel well enough to go? You look as if you could use a brandy.'

'Yes, I do. And yes, I could.' She answered as lightly as possible.

He closed her door, and a moment later slid behind the wheel and reached over to fasten her seat belt.

Though he glanced at her from time to time, as if to reassure himself, Jos didn't speak until they were drawing up in the car park at the Barley Mow.

'Would you prefer to sit inside or outside?'

Normally Clare would have preferred to sit outside, but the garden, where wooden tables and benches jostled for a place in the sun, appeared to be crowded with tourists.

'Inside, I think.'

His arm firmly around her waist, they went into the comparative gloom of the lounge, which was practically empty except for a small group of men clustered by the bar exchanging banter with the bartender.

The place smelled of coffee, bitter beer and the lemon-scented geraniums that stood in pots on the deep window sills.

Having seated Clare at a small corner table, Jos went

to the bar. She noticed that, though he made no effort to attract attention, even in the casual trousers and cotton polo-neck he had presence enough to make the bartender immediately leave the group and hurry over.

Carrying a double brandy for her and a half-pint of bitter for himself, he returned quite quickly. He still looked taut, she thought, the planes and angles of his face sharp beneath the tanned skin.

Eyeing the brandy he'd placed in front of her, Clare remarked ruefully, 'If I drink all that on an empty stomach I'll have to be carried to the car a second time.'

Jos grinned briefly, as she'd hoped he would, and told her, 'There's a plate of beef sandwiches coming.'

She was still sipping the brandy when they arrived.

They ate in silence—Jos like a man with a great deal on his mind, Clare with an appetite that surprised her.

They were each drinking coffee before he remarked, 'You look better. You're starting to get a trace of colour back.'

'I feel better, and I'm glad I finally know the worst...' she said, and in a low voice she added, 'But why did your mother commit suicide in *our* house?'

'Do you remember which room she came out of?'

'Yes...' Clare whispered. 'My mother had had two bedrooms converted into a sitting room-cum-study on the top floor. She loved the view from the windows and said she didn't get disturbed up there when she settled down to write letters. In those days she was an avid correspondent. But why should your mother...?'

'I can only presume she'd been to have it out with Isobel, to ask her to give Charles up. When Isobel refused, I suppose my mother couldn't bear the thought of losing the man she was devoted to. Perhaps, on the spur of the moment, it seemed preferable to end it...'

Clare shuddered. 'That's *never* the way. Things change, situations alter. There's no sense in deliberately throwing your life away...'

'I agree.'

'Are you *sure* she did?'

'You were there.'

'But I'd never heard any mention of divorce, and I just thought your mother's fall was a dreadful accident... As surely it *must* have been? Those balustrades are very low...'

'They're at least waist-high, he corrected.

'I thought they were a good foot lower than that...and it seemed to me she stumbled.. ' Clare shuddered again at the memory. 'The first time I showed you round Stratton Place—I relived everything then, though I didn't appreciate you were Clave. I was horrified...'

'Yes, I know. Your face turned as white as paper and I thought you were going to faint. But it was obvious you didn't recognise me, and when I asked what was wrong, you just said you weren't feeling well.'

'That day in Central Park...when you were talking about looking round houses...it was that half-remembered recollection that frightened me so much. And I suppose that's what scared me today. But for some reason I wasn't expecting it to be Stratton Place...'

'You thought it was the Priory?'

'Yes. Even though you said you'd looked at *two* houses, it didn't occur to me that Stratton Place was the other one...'

A thought struck her, and she asked, 'Jos, why did you want to leave going there until the afternoon?'

'The first time we looked at the houses it was in the same order, and at about the same time of day, with the sun coming through those high windows...'

'And you wanted the conditions to be different?'

'I was afraid of what the shock of remembering might do to you. I wanted you to get your memory back—you seemed only half alive without it—but I didn't want you to remember that particular incident. I got the impression that you'd managed to block it out of your mind until that first time you took me round.'

'I had. You see, after that awful day I could hardly bear to be in the house. For a long time I had bad dreams and waking nightmares. The doctor called it some kind of neurosis... You obviously didn't know, but until then I'd secretly hero-worshipped you, and longed for your approval. Then afterwards, when I thought you might be going to live with us, I couldn't bear it. You were so much part of that terrible memory—a memory I *had* to get away from somehow... That's why I behaved as I did. When it was too late, and I realised what I'd done, I felt ashamed, bitterly sorry...

'You once told me my parents pushed me off to boarding-school. But that wasn't so. I *asked* to go... After I went, gradually the nightmares and the feelings of guilt stopped, and I was able to bury the memory in my subconscious. The only thing that remained was my fear of heights...

'I never went back home after that, not even for holidays. My parents had a flat in town, and if they were going to be there I joined them. If not, I made arrangements to stay with one or other of my friends. And when the time came to finally leave school, I could have lived at Stratton Place but I knew I didn't want to. I told myself it was because I liked the idea of being totally independent.

'Though I prefer the country I'd half decided to try and find a job and a bedsit in London when Graham

Ashleigh offered me a job with his firm. He also made arrangements for me to rent Mr Drury's cottage...'

Jos's mouth moved in a smile that was more of a sneer. 'He sounds like a Mr Fix-it.'

Stiffly, she said, 'Graham was an old family friend.'

'And a would-be lover? Despite the fact that he was a widower and lot older than you?'

With touch of malice, she informed him, 'He's only four years older than you are.'

'Would you have become Mrs Ashleigh the second if I hadn't come along?' Again there was that curl of the lip.

'I don't know,' she admitted truthfully. 'I might have done...'

Judging by the glitter in Jos's green eyes, that wasn't what he'd wanted to hear.

'We'd been out together quite a lot and we were fond of each other.'

'*Fond!*' Jos echoed derisively. 'The man was besotted; he could barely keep his hands off you.'

For a moment or two the realisation that Jos was jealous gave Clare a lift, but common sense soon pointed out that you didn't have to be in love to be jealous, only possessive.

Suddenly, unexpectedly, she yawned.

Jos's eyes narrowed. 'It's time we got you back to bed.'

'Bed? But it's only two-thirty.' Despite her protestation, she yawned again.

'Come on.' With an arm around her, he half lifted her. 'Tiredness can be one of the signs of delayed shock.'

'It's more likely to be the brandy.'

Whatever the cause, half an hour later she was in bed. Jos drew the flowered curtains across the open window to shut out most of the brightness and stooped to kiss her lightly. 'Try to get some sleep.'

For a moment the kiss and his obvious concern warmed her, and spun a thread of hope for the future. But what chance had they of finding any kind of happiness together when he was convinced that *her* mother was responsible for *his* mother's suicide?

If it had been suicide. Somehow she couldn't believe it.

Eyes closed, mentally bracing herself, she deliberately relived those few seconds, seeing again that slim hurrying figure, the stumble, the thigh-height balustrade...

The *thigh-height* balustrade...

But Jos had said *waist-height*. One of them had to be wrong... Her thoughts were getting blurred and she was too tired to decide which...

A second later she was fast asleep.

Jos stood gazing down at her, on his lean face a look of such tenderness that Clare would have been transfixed had she seen it.

She looked childishly innocent, he thought, and frighteningly vulnerable. One hand was lying on the pillow beside her dark head, palm up, fingers slightly curled, showing the oval nails with their natural shine.

Her heart-shaped face was still wan, and the long lashes, spread like fans, failed to disguise the mauve shadows beneath her eyes. Her lips were pale and her flawless skin looked almost translucent.

But, fragile as she seemed, he knew now that she had grown up with strength and courage, an inner core of steel that made her a fighter. Made her able to face life, to look tragedy in the face and then put it behind her.

He touched her cheek in a gentle caress, before going quietly out.

Clare awoke to immediate and complete remembrance, her mind oddly clear and lucid. A glance at her watch showed she'd slept for almost two hours.

While she'd slept her subconscious had been busy. Knowing now what she had to do, she jumped out of bed and, pulling on the cotton skirt and button-through top and the sandals she'd taken off earlier, hurried downstairs.

There was no sign of Jos. Opening the window, Clare stuck her head out and looked towards the parking area. The hired car was missing.

Jos had obviously gone somewhere, but the keys to both the houses—probably because they'd weighed his pocket down—had been left on the coffee-table, along with the spare keys to Lamb Cottage.

Dropping the keys to Stratton Place and Lamb Cottage into her shoulder-bag, Clare let herself out and walked the two hundred yards to where George Hammet, who drove the village taxi, lived.

There was no sign of either George or his vehicle.

She was wondering whether to set off on the two-mile walk to Stratton Place when the obvious solution struck her. Before her marriage, often needing to take clients to view properties, she'd had the use of one or other of Ashleigh Kent's cars, and she had no doubt that Graham would lend her one now, if one was available.

Crossing the green, abstractedly enjoying the smell of the newly mown grass, she made her way up Yeoman Street and pushed open the door to the estate agents.

Graham, impeccably dressed as usual, his fair hair neatly brushed, was coming the opposite way and they met in the doorway. He was a big man, almost as tall as Jos and considerably heavier. He'd been a Rugby Union forward in his younger days.

'Clare!' His good-looking, somewhat heavy face lit up. 'How nice to see you...' Then, 'Oh, hell! I'm just on my way out; I've an urgent appointment.'

'That's all right.' She smiled up at him. 'I only came to ask if I could borrow a car for an hour. Jos has taken ours.'

'I'm afraid all the cars are out. Where did you want to get to?'

'Stratton Place. I...I went there this morning, but I need to go again...'

He beamed his relief. 'My appointment's at Copthorn. I can easily drop you at the house and pick you up on the way back, if that will suit you?'

'That's ideal.'

When they were in the sleek Jaguar, heading out of the village, he glanced at her, his blue eyes troubled. 'Is everything working out all right? I mean...well, you do love Saunders, don't you?'

'Everything's fine. And, yes, I do love him.'

'I suppose I shouldn't have asked, only you're not looking too well.'

'I think it must be the heat.' Then, realising he knew quite well that she could stand any amount of heat, she asked hurriedly, 'So how are things at this end? How's the real estate business?'

'Could be worse. Buyers are still a bit cautious, but we've several parties interested in Stratton Place...'

Graham had always been an enthusiastic talker, and while he launched into an account of the various possibilities Clare allowed part of her mind to wander, listening with one ear.

When she'd first taken Jos to view Foxton Priory and Stratton Place, some four months previously, it had been in this self-same car.

Remembering that drive now, she could recall how much just sitting beside him had affected her. Overwhelmingly conscious of that powerfully attractive face, that lean, muscular body, that potent sexuality, her pulse had raced and her cheeks had been unusually flushed.

Aware that Jos had turned a little in his seat and was studying her profile with great deliberation, she'd stared resolutely ahead, doing her best to keep her attention on the road but feeling the betraying flush deepen.

'Warm?' he'd teased.

She'd given him an angry glance and, seeing the amusement gleaming in his green eyes, inviting her to laugh with him, had succumbed then and there to his charm.

He'd been irresistible, and every instinct she'd possessed had been warning her that he was also *dangerous*. The knowledge had scared her half to death.

Instead of laughing with him, she'd armoured herself with that cool composure he'd talked about. But, against what she now recognised as a determined assault, it had proved as ineffectual as glass armour...

'And the contract could be signed as soon as you've decided whether or not you want to part with the contents,' Graham wound up as they stopped by the steps at Stratton Place.

Anxious not to make him late, Clare scrambled out and thanked him with a smile.

'I'll pick you up in about an hour,' he told her, and as soon as she'd closed the car door accelerated away down the tree-lined drive.

Overcoming her nervous qualms, her sudden fear of going in alone, Clare opened the door and forced herself to walk over the threshold.

Expecting to be met by dark memories and ghosts of the past, she found neither. Facing them had apparently put them to flight.

The hall was bare and beautiful, the air a little musty, the atmosphere innocuous. Its only furnishings were a long oak table, a matching settle and several heavy metal-bound chests that Clare knew had always stood there.

Bracing herself, she looked up at the galleries. Jos had been right; the balustrades were at least waist-height. But her conviction that they had been a lot lower was so strong that her mind would scarcely believe the evidence of her own eyes.

Of course, it was still possible that his mother's fall had been accidental. Though less likely.

Her footsteps sounding loud in the silence, Clare took the right-hand staircase up to the second gallery and opened the door into what had been her mother's sitting-room-cum-study.

It was light and spacious, furnished with carefully chosen antiques. Only the comfortable armchairs and the curtains looked modern. Between the two windows stood a beautiful walnut bureau, and she had a sudden vivid picture of her mother, wearing something blue, sitting writing at that desk.

She couldn't have been much more than four at the time, and Nanny had brought her in to say goodnight. She'd asked, What are you writing? She could almost hear her own childish treble, and her mother's slightly husky voice answering, 'My diary. I always write down everything that happens to me and then I don't forget.'

Sitting down at the bureau, feeling a kind of silent communication with her, Clare thought about her mother. They had never been close, but she still felt sure in her own mind that though Isobel might have been weak and amoral she hadn't been wicked.

Obeying an impulse, Clare began to look through the drawers, searching for something, anything, that might back up that certainty.

One was full of letters and personal papers, another packed with a jumble of household bills and receipts. A third held several piles of leather-bound diaries.

Surely a diary, that most intimate confidant, would reveal a person's true character...

Hands a little unsteady, Clare went through them. Finding the year she was looking for, and unaware of the shock that was in store for her, she started to read.

She'd almost reached the end when the sound of a car horn jolted her back to the present. Stumbling to the window, she looked down and saw Graham's Jaguar waiting for her.

Putting the diary into her bag, she walked along the gallery, careful not to look over, and down the stairs, holding onto the handrail. She felt sick and agitated, stomach churning, thoughts in a whirl.

Graham got out of the car to open her door. 'I hope you don't think I'm rushing you, but I've got another early evening appointment and—'

He broke off at the sight of her strained white face and exclaimed, 'God, you look terrible! Are you sure you're not ill?'

It seemed easier not to explain, just to say, 'Perhaps I'm coming down with summer flu. I'll have a cup of tea and a lie-down when I get back.'

Once settled in the car, reluctant to talk, she rested her head against the back of the seat and closed her eyes.

When they reached Lamb Cottage there was still no sign of the hired car. 'Jos isn't back yet.' She voiced the thought aloud.

Graham frowned, and, clearly concerned about her, said, 'I'll see you in.'

She made no demur, and with an arm about her waist he walked with her to the door and opened it for her.

'If you'd like to go straight to bed, I'll bring you up a cup of tea before I dash off.'

Without waiting for an answer, he followed her in and went through to the kitchen.

Feeling ashamed that all she really wanted was for him to go and leave her to think, Clare tossed her bag aside and took off her sandals.

The door had been left ajar and the scent of roses and honeysuckle drifted in, their combined scent filling the air.

Graham returned to say, 'The kettle's on. Do you want an aspirin or anything?'

'No, I'll be fine, thank you.' Grateful for his kindness, she raised herself on tiptoe to kiss his cheek and, standing on one of the discarded sandals, wobbled a little.

Putting an arm around her waist to steady her, he asked, 'Would you like me to help you upstairs…?'

'No, she wouldn't, Ashleigh! Or rather, *she* might, but *I* wouldn't.'

'Jos!' Clare exclaimed as they sprang apart.

Tall and dark, his face taut above the black polo-neck, an angry glitter in his green eyes, Jos seemed to dominate the small room.

Thrown, because she knew they must have looked guilty, Clare stammered, 'I—I didn't hear you come in.'

'That's quite obvious.' Jos's voice was icy. Turning to Graham, he ordered with quiet menace, 'Get the hell out of here! If I catch you within a mile of my wife again, I'll break your neck.'

'You don't understand,' Clare cried desperately. 'Graham was only trying to help…'

As though she hadn't spoken, his eyes fixed on the other man, Jos went on, 'In fact, if you don't move fast I might be tempted to do it right now.'

Standing his ground, Graham began, 'Now, you just listen to me, Saunders, you've got it all wrong…'

At the same instant Clare begged, 'Jos, please don't do anything you might regret…'

But with a dangerous gleam in his eyes Jos was advancing on the other man, while Graham, recovered from being startled, was now looking distinctly belligerent, his heavy face darkly flushed.

Realising she had no chance of physically stopping the pair, Clare put a hand to her head and with a low moan pitched forward into Jos's arms.

He gave a little grunt as he caught and supported her weight.

In the split second that followed both men glared at each other. Then, muttering, 'Oh, hell!' Graham headed for the door.

In the doorway he turned. 'Everything was completely innocent, so for God's sake don't take it out on Clare.' A second later the door banged behind him.

Supporting Clare's inert figure with one arm, Jos pulled open the door to the stairs and carried her up to the bedroom. Then, setting her on her feet, gripping her upper arms, he said grimly, 'Right, you can quit the play-acting. I know a genuine faint from a phoney.'

Lifting her head, Clare opened her eyes and sighed.

'It wouldn't have been necessary if you hadn't jumped to conclusions. You know you were quite mistaken—'

'Mistaken be damed! When I find my wife in another man's arms, kissing him, and hear that the next move is upstairs...' He ground his teeth. 'Obviously I'm not keeping you satisfied. Well, if it's sex you're in need of...'

'Jos, I—'

'Take your clothes off.'

'Don't talk to me like that,' she flared.

'Think yourself lucky I'm only talking.'

'Perhaps you'd like to beat me?'

'I'm tempted. But I haven't struck a female since I was thirteen and I don't intend to start again now. There are other ways of reinforcing my ownership.'

As he spoke he was stripping off his clothes.

Her eyes were riveted to the masculine perfection of his naked body, the broad chest with its plates of muscle layering the ribcage, the bunched power of shoulders and biceps, the narrow waist and lean hips, the long, straight legs.

He was beautiful...

Her soft mouth firmed. But that didn't mean she was going to allow him to ride roughshod over her.

His hands moved suddenly, and she gasped as her cotton top was wrenched apart, the buttons torn forcibly through the buttonholes.

'I said, take your clothes off. Unless you want me to do it for you.'

Her expression mutinous, she stood silently, making no move to obey.

He smiled sardonically. 'You do like playing with fire, don't you?'

As soon as he touched her she started to fight, kicking

and scratching, striking out at him fiercely. But despite her struggles, using swift, decisive movements, bothering with neither buttons nor hooks, he tore off the rest of her clothing.

The next instant she found herself spread-eagled on the bed and Jos bending over her, his hands and knees trapping her there.

For a while his mouth roved over her breasts, playing with the sensitive nipples, then, to give himself more scope, he brought her hands down, pinning them by her sides.

'I hate you!' she muttered fiercely.

He laughed while his mouth moved over her flat stomach and the silken skin of her inner thighs and drove her slowly wild.

Eyes closed, turning her head restlessly from side to side, hands clenching and unclenching, she groaned as his lips and teeth and tongue wrung from her an intensity of stimulation that was akin to torture.

It was almost a relief when she felt the weight of his body settle on hers. Despite his threats he was gentle with her until, showing one last spark of defiance, she sank her teeth into his shoulder, then, with fire and arrogance, a fierce, driving passion, his body made itself master of hers.

Engulfed by a rapture so pure and intense that it was almost pain, she cried silently, I love you. Oh, I love you...

Then Jos's hands gripping her, Jos's voice demanding fiercely, 'Who do you love?' cut short the bliss.

'What?' she asked dazedly.

'Who do you love?'

'You. I love you.'

Looking shaken, he said, 'You sound as if you mean it.'

She turned her head so that her face was pressed against the brown column of his throat. 'I *do* mean it. I've loved you from the first moment I saw you. Even when I couldn't *remember*, I knew I loved you.'

'In spite of everything?' He sounded stunned.

'In spite of everything.'

'Then what was Ashleigh doing here? Why were you kissing him?'

Briefly, she explained.

'You went back to Stratton Place *alone*? But why?'

'I wanted to take another look at the balustrades. I found they were waist-high, as you said, but I *remembered* them as being lower—the kind they used to have in minstrels' galleries...'

'And you were right.'

'How do you know that?'

'I went into town, to the *Gazette* offices, and asked to see back copies of the paper. I found the one with the story of what they called THE FATAL PLUNGE.

'The coroner's verdict was accidental death, and it was suggested that the low balustrade and the fact that the victim had been drinking heavily prior to the accident had been the main contributory factors. He further suggested that to prevent any further tragedies the balustrades should be replaced by higher ones...'

'And they were. My mother recorded it in her diary.'

'She kept a personal diary?' Jos asked sharply.

Clare nodded.

'Did she go into detail about what happened and why?'

'Yes, it's all there. But it might be better not to read it, just to let the past go.'

His face tight, he said, 'If you're trying to protect her—'

'I'm not.'

'In any case, I think I have a right to know.'

'Very well. The diary's in my bag, downstairs. I'll get it.'

When he'd been reading for some ten minutes, his face pale beneath the tan, Jos looked up to say slowly, 'So it was *me* you were trying to protect.' Then, 'God! All these years I've been hating the wrong woman...' His knuckles gleamed white as he clenched his hands.

'There's no need to hate anyone,' Clare said urgently. 'Especially not yourself.'

'How could I have been so wrong?' He sounded agonised.

She touched his cheek. 'You were young when you overheard your parents quarrelling, talking about a divorce. It wasn't your fault that you misinterpreted what you heard...'

'I didn't misinterpret it so much as turn the whole thing back to front... But even as a child I could see how bewitching Isobel was, and my own mother had always seemed such a devoted wife...'

There was a long pause before he went on, 'I'd never dreamt of my mother falling so deeply in love with another man that she'd want a divorce...'

Clare sighed. 'Neither had my father, apparently. As far as *he* was concerned, your mother was just another one of his affairs. The last thing he wanted was a divorce, in case it ruined his career. Strange how two women could have kept loving a man like that.

'Though it's clear no one doubted that your mother's death was an accident, it must have been the realisation of what kind of man my father really was, how he'd just *used* her, that made her drink too much. And you saw what it did to my own mother… So if anyone's responsible for wrecking so many lives, it's my father…'

'You once remarked that it takes two to tango,' Jos said quietly, 'and I've since realised you were right. My mother must at least share the responsibility.'

After a moment, Clare said, 'The only thing I can be happy about is that despite everything our mothers stayed friends until the end.'

Jos sighed. 'Can you ever forgive me for laying all the blame at Isobel's door?'

'If you hadn't, we wouldn't be where we are now,' Clare pointed out.

'And where are we now?' He sounded weary.

Ignoring the deeper meaning, she answered, 'In bed together.'

'Is that where you want to be?'

'It is.'

She saw the flare of hope in his green eyes as he asked, 'Then, generally speaking, you're happy with the way things are?'

'They're *almost* perfect.'

'So what do you need to make them *absolutely* perfect?'

'A marriage that will last until we're old.'

'I've always intended it to. Anything else?'

'A real home in the country.'

'Could you bring yourself to like the Priory?'

'I already do. In fact it was love at first sight.'

'Then we'll make that our home. Anything else?'

A shade hesitantly, she suggested, 'It's a house that cries out for a big, happy family…'

'Children?' He raised a dark brow. 'How many were you thinking of?'

'Three or four.'

'I guess we could manage that. Anything else?'

'Perhaps—for when we visit New York—a penthouse with a butler who plays poker and drinks bourbon.'

'That you already have. Anything else?'

For a moment she was silent, then she admitted, 'Most of all, I'd like you to like me.'

He said, as he'd said once before, 'Liking is such a bloodless, insipid emotion. Would you settle for enough deep, passionate love to last a lifetime?'

Violet eyes brimming with tears, she whispered, 'I might.'

'Then it's yours.' Holding her close, he kissed away the tears. 'It always has been.'

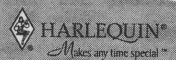

Take 2 bestselling love stories FREE

Plus get a FREE surprise gift!

Special Limited-Time Offer

Mail to Harlequin Reader Service®

3010 Walden Avenue
P.O. Box 1867
Buffalo, N.Y. 14240-1867

YES! Please send me 2 free Harlequin Presents® novels and my free surprise gift. Then send me 6 brand-new novels every month, which I will receive months before they appear in bookstores. Bill me at the low price of $3.12 each plus 25¢ delivery and applicable sales tax, if any*. That's the complete price, and a saving of over 10% off the cover prices—quite a bargain! I understand that accepting the books and gift places me under no obligation ever to buy any books. I can always return a shipment and cancel at any time. Even if I never buy another book from Harlequin, the 2 free books and the surprise gift are mine to keep forever.

106 HEN CH69

Name	(PLEASE PRINT)	
Address	Apt. No.	
City	State	Zip

This offer is limited to one order per household and not valid to present Harlequin Presents® subscribers. *Terms and prices are subject to change without notice. Sales tax applicable in N.Y.

UPRES-98   ©1990 Harlequin Enterprises Limited

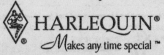

Toast the special events in your life with Harlequin Presents®!

With the purchase of *two* Harlequin Presents®
BIG EVENT books, you can send in for two sparkling
plum-colored Wineglasses. A retail value of $19.95!

ACT NOW TO COLLECT
TWO BEAUTIFUL WINEGLASSES!

On the official proof-of-purchase coupon below, fill in your name,
address and zip or postal code and send it, plus $2.99 U.S./$3.99 CAN.
for postage and handling (check or money order—please do not send
cash) payable to Harlequin Books, to: In the U.S.: 3010 Walden
Avenue, P.O. Box 9077, Buffalo, N.Y. 14269-9077; In Canada: P.O. Box
609, Fort Erie, Ontario L2A 5X3. Please allow 4-6 weeks for delivery.
Order your set of wineglasses now! Quantities are limited. Offer for
the Plum Wineglasses expires December 31, 1998.

Harlequin Presents®—The Big Event!

OFFICIAL PROOF OF PURCHASE

"Please send me my TWO Wineglasses"

Name: _____

Address: _____

City: _____

State/Prov.: _____ Zip/Postal Code: _____

Account Number: _____ 097 KGS CSA6 193-3

HPBEPOP

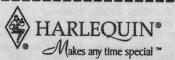

HARLEQUIN®
Makes any time special ™

Coming Next Month

HARLEQUIN PRESENTS®

THE BEST HAS JUST GOTTEN BETTER!

#1995 MARRIED BY CHRISTMAS Carole Mortimer
Lilli was mortified when she woke up in Patrick Devlin's bed! He wasn't about to let her forget it, either. Patrick would save her father's chain of hotels...if she married him—by Christmas!

#1996 THE BRIDAL BED Helen Bianchin
(Do Not Disturb)
For her mother's wedding, Suzanne and her ex-fiancé, Sloan, had to play the part of a happy, soon-to-marry couple! After sharing a room—and a bed!—their pretend passion became real...and another wedding was on the agenda!

#1997 BABY INCLUDED! Mary Lyons
(The Big Event!)
Lord Ratcliffe was delighted that Eloise had turned up at his surprise birthday party. He'd always thought she was an ordinary American tourist; but in fact she was an international sex symbol...and secretly carrying his baby!

#1998 A HUSBAND'S PRICE Diana Hamilton
Six years ago when Adam and Claudia had split up, he'd left a part of himself with her—a child. Now Adam's help comes with a hefty price tag—that Claudia become his wife. Faced with bankruptcy and a custody battle, Claudia has no choice....

#1999 A NANNY FOR CHRISTMAS Sara Craven
(Nanny Wanted!)
Dominic Ashton thought Phoebe was a wonderful stand-in mom for little Tara; it was a pity she couldn't stay longer. But Phoebe had her reasons for going: if Dominic had forgotten their first meeting years before, she certainly hadn't!

#2000 MORGAN'S CHILD Anne Mather
(Harlequin Presents' 2000th title!)
Four years after the death of her husband in war-torn Africa, Felicity Riker at last had a new man...a new life. Then she heard that Morgan had been found *alive*...and that he was on his was back to reclaim his long-lost wife....